ALLIE FINKLE

RULES

FOR

GIRLS

STAGE FRIGHT

Meg Cabot is the author of the phenomenally successful The Princess Diaries series. With vast numbers of copies sold around the world, the books have topped the US and UK bestseller lists for weeks and won several awards. Two movies based on the series have been massively popular throughout the world.

Meg is also the author of the bestselling Airhead trilogy, the Abandon trilogy, *All-American Girl*, *All-American Girl: Ready or Not*, *How to Be Popular*, *Jinx*, *Teen Idol*, *Avalon High*, *Tommy Sullivan Is a Freak*, The Mediator series and the Allie Finkle series as well as many other books for teenagers and adults. She and her husband divide their time between New York and Florida.

Visit Meg Cabot's website at
www.megcabot.co.uk

Books by Meg Cabot

The Allie Finkle series
Moving Day
The New Girl
Best Friends and Drama Queens
Stage Fright
Glitter Girls
Blast from the Past

For teens
The Princess Diaries series
The Mediator series
The Airhead trilogy
The Abandon trilogy
All-American Girl
All-American Girl: Ready or Not
Avalon High
Teen Idol
How to Be Popular
Jinx
Tommy Sullivan Is a Freak
Nicola and the Viscount
Victoria and the Rogue

ALLIE FINKLE'S
RULES
FOR
GIRLS

STAGE FRIGHT

MEG CABOT

MACMILLAN CHILDREN'S BOOKS

First published 2009 by Macmillan Children's Books

This edition published 2010 by Macmillan Children's Books
a division of Macmillan Publishers Limited
20 New Wharf Road, London N1 9RR
Basingstoke and Oxford
Associated companies throughout the world
www.panmacmillan.com

ISBN 978-0-330-45378-3

5 7 9 8 6

A CIP catalogue record for this book is available from
the British Library.

Typeset by Intype Libra Ltd
Printed and bound by CPI Group (UK) Ltd, Croydon, CR0 4YY

For Every Reader with a Dream

Many thanks to Beth Ader, Jennifer Brown, Barbara Cabot, Michele Jaffe, Laura Langlie, Abigail McAden, Fliss Stevens and especially Benjamin Egnatz

Rule #1

It's Important to Try to Make
Your Friends Feel Good About
Themselves As Often As Possible.
Then They'll Like You Better

What's amazing is how you can be a normal kid one day and then something happens that completely changes your life.

I mean it. One minute you're just an average, ordinary kind of girl . . . not boring, of course, because you're good at maths and science and an excellent big sister to two pretty horrible little brothers – not to mention a really good owner to a kitten, because you want to be a veterinarian some day – but not particularly amazing either . . . and then something comes along that changes everything.

Not like aliens coming down in a spaceship and telling you that you are their long-lost queen and they've been combing the galaxy looking for you for years and that that weird freckle on your elbow is actually a homing beacon and proves you're one of them.

And then they ask you to come back with them to Planet Voltron, where everything is made out of candy and you will be the Voltrons' leader and you'll have a pet unicorn with wings and get to be a veterinarian without actually having to go through four years of college plus four years of veterinary school plus an additional three- to four-year residency, the amount of time it takes to become a board-certified veterinarian on Planet Earth.

Although that would be very, very cool.

But I mean like your mom suddenly becoming a TV star.

And OK, my mom isn't exactly a TV *star*.

'I just got a part-time job as the movie reviewer for that local cable show *Good News!*,' she explained that night when she got home from her other part-time job as a college adviser (she advises college students what kind of classes to take. For instance, computer classes, which is what my dad teaches at the same college).

At first there was stunned silence when Mom said this. Because none of us even knew Mom was trying out for the job of movie reviewer on *Good News!*, which, by the way, is super famous. Not in the whole world or anything. I mean, Grandma had never heard

2

of it when she came to visit. *Good News!* is only on our local cable channel 4.

But still, it's super famous in our town. My best friend Erica has even been on it. *Good News!* came to her gymnastics studio once and filmed everyone doing their routines before the big statewide gymnastics championship (which Erica wasn't in, but they showed her giving chalk to a girl who was practising for it and who came in twentieth).

And Erica's big sister, Missy, has been on *Good News!* lots of times, because Missy is a majorette in the marching band at the middle school, and *Good News!* is always showing stuff like the local marching-band competitions, and once even the pie-eating competition at the county fair, which Erica's older brother John was in (only he got disqualified when Erica's mom found out and told the judges he had a wheat-gluten allergy).

Good News! comes on right after the regular news. It even stars one of the same newsreaders as the regular news, Lynn Martinez. She just takes off the glasses she wears while doing the news, changes into a more sparkly shirt, messes up her hair and, suddenly, the regular news turns into *Good News!* at seven o'clock. So you can forget all about all the bad news you just heard, and concentrate on the good news Lynn is about to tell you, like about what restaurants are opening up in town, or what new plays you can see at the community theatre, or how somebody's cat is nursing a poor orphaned baby deer back to health, or how somebody else is having a sneaker drive to raise sneakers for poor people in Africa who can't afford their own sneakers.

See? It's all *good news*. That's why they call it *Good News!*

And my mom was going to be on it! The best show on TV!

I know. Is that fantastic or what? I am the daughter of a celebrity.

'Elizabeth,' Dad said, looking proud but a little surprised, 'I had no idea you were interested in tele-journalism.'

'Oh, well,' Mom said, fluffing her hair out after taking off her coat, 'I saw the ad in the paper and I thought it looked like it might be fun, so I applied. You know I reviewed films for our school paper in college. It's going to be a little different reading them on camera, but the idea's basically the same. I'm excited to get back to reviewing.'

And OK, maybe Mom's not a celebrity exactly, because *Good News!* isn't shown all around the whole country.

But it still seems pretty obvious that because of

Mom's new job my life will never be normal again. It won't be long before the paparazzi start showing up at our house. Maybe we'll even have to get bodyguards! I mean, when your mom works for *Good News!*, that is a very big deal.

'The truth is, I suspect I'm the only person who tried out,' Mom said, 'because they hired me as soon as they saw my audition. I have a feeling this town isn't exactly crawling with wannabe local-cable-news-show film reviewers.'

Except that this isn't true. The reason my mom got the job is that she's the coolest, most beautiful mom there is. I know this because I've met a lot of other kids' moms.

And OK, my ex-best friend Mary Kay Shiner's mom had a very fancy job at a law firm and was always saying things into her cellphone like, 'Nancy, I needed those depositions yesterday!'

And my other ex-friend Brittany Hauser's mom has a show cat named Lady Serena Archibald and very fancy high-heeled shoes with feathers on them.

But neither of them is as cool as my mom, who is restoring an old house to make it nice again (even if she's taking a really long time about it, if you ask me. Though my room is the nicest room of all my friends', and when they come over and see it for the first time they totally freak out over my wallpaper and lace curtains).

So, you know.

'That's not true,' Dad said about Mom's joke that no one else had applied. He was setting out the takeaway pizza Mom had brought home for dinner to celebrate her new job. The pizza came from Pizza Express, which happens to be where my Uncle Jay has a job. Even though Uncle Jay's girlfriend, Harmony, didn't think so at first, being a delivery man for Pizza Express has turned out to be the best job ever for Uncle Jay. He gets to eat all the pizzas they give him the wrong addresses for – for free!

Only tonight, even though Uncle Jay had come over for dinner, we were having pizza we had actually paid for, since it was a special occasion.

'I'm sure a lot of talented people applied for that job,' Dad told Mom. 'You just happened to have had the best audition. The reviews you wrote in college were wonderful. You've always had very keen insight into the world of media and entertainment.'

'Yeah, Mom,' I said, scraping the tomato sauce off my pizza slice from underneath the melted cheese. Because one of my rules is, *Never eat anything red.* Frankly I prefer white pizza, but since I'm the only one in the family who does, I only get that kind of pizza when Uncle Jay delivers one to someone and it turns out Pizza Express messed up and it's not the kind they actually ordered. 'You always have a lot to say about *Hannah Montana*.'

'Well,' Mom said, 'I guess you might be right.'

'What's the first movie you're going to review?' Uncle Jay wanted to know. Uncle Jay doesn't live with us, but he's always hanging around, even though he has a girlfriend and a job and studies at the university.

Mom looked at the paper the people at *Good News!* had given her. 'Something called *Requiem for a Somnambulist*,' she said.

'Ouch,' Uncle Jay said, I guess because *Requiem for a Somnambulist* didn't sound so good to him. It didn't sound so good to me either, to tell the truth.

'Wow,' Dad said, 'I'm sure you'll have plenty to say about that one.'

'Are we going to get to be on TV too?' my little brother Kevin wanted to know.

'Why would *we* get to be on Mom's show?' My other little brother, Mark, was chewing with his mouth open, as was his custom. Also speaking with his mouth full of food, violating two of my rules, *Don't chew with your mouth open* and *Swallow what's in your mouth before speaking*. Having two little brothers who won't

7

follow the rules of common courtesy at meal times makes my life a constant trial.

'Lots of times the kids of movie stars get to be on TV,' Kevin said. 'Like when they go to movie premieres.'

I hadn't even thought about movie premieres! But obviously we were going to get to go to lots of those. Movie critics always get to see movies before anyone else does. They have to. How else are they going to warn people not to see the bad ones? We were probably going to meet tons of stars. Such as Miley Cyrus.

'I'm not going to be invited to movie premieres, honey,' Mom said. '*Good News!* is not that big a TV show. It's just on the local station. And besides, most movie premieres are held in Hollywood, and we live very far from there.'

This was really disappointing to hear. Because the truth was, I was totally thinking, just like Kevin was, that I might get to be on Mom's TV show too. Or that at the very least my whole life would change now that I was the daughter of a famous TV film critic, and not simply the daughter of a college adviser and a college professor.

Not that there is anything wrong with those two jobs. It's just that they are sort of boring compared to being a TV star.

STAGE FRIGHT

When I went to bed that night, I told my kitten, Mewsie – who is actually growing really fast and weighs six pounds now, which is exceptional for his age according to our vet, Dr DeLorenzo – that it looked like our chances of hitting the big time were pretty much zero.

'Guess you're just going to be plain old Mewsie,' I told him as he lay purring on my chest, his nightly routine. It's very hard to sleep that way, but it's still nice. 'Instead of Mewsie, Celebrity Kitten.'

But when I told my best friends, Erica, Sophie and Caroline, my mom's news on the way to school the next day, they all had a different opinion about it.

'I bet she'll have you on as a guest,' Sophie said. 'Like when she reviews kids' movies.'

'Wow,' I said. I had never thought of this, 'do you really think so?'

'Oh, of course,' Sophie said. 'If she's any good at her job, she'll want to get the opinion of the target audience. Obviously.' We knew all about target audiences from Erica's big sister Missy's teen magazines, which Missy never exactly let us borrow, but we snuck them from her room whenever she was away at a band competition or in the bathroom experimenting with a new pimple medication.

Sophie made me feel excited again about my mom's

new job. Even more excited than I would have been about finding out I was actually queen of an alien race. Because, Sophie said when I told her about it – and Caroline and Erica agreed – having a mom who reviews movies on TV is more interesting than being queen of an alien race. Because it's more realistic.

'You're so lucky,' Erica said with a sigh. 'I wish my mom had her own TV show. But she doesn't do anything except run her own store of fine collectables.'

'What about my mom,' Caroline said with a sigh. 'She's only dean of a women's college. In *Maine*.'

We all agreed this was a terrible occupation compared to my mom's new job.

'Maybe my mom will have all of us on her show,' I said. I was just saying this to be nice. I didn't really believe Mom would have me and all my friends on her TV show some day. *It's important to try to make your friends feel good about themselves as often as possible. Then they'll like you better.* This is a rule.

'When I go on Mom's TV show, I'm going to wear velvet pants,' Kevin said. I have to walk Kevin to school every day (and home from school too) because he's only in kindergarten and I'm the oldest. It's OK though, because all the fifth-grade girls think Kevin is really cute, so having him around has helped me to look cool in front of them.

'Whatever, Kevin,' I said. He doesn't even own a pair of velvet pants, though he begs for them all the time. The closest he's come is corduroys, which he pretends are velvet.

'We should start planning what we're going to wear though,' Sophie said, ignoring Kevin, 'just in case. I have some totally cool leggings with silver spider webs printed on them left over from Halloween, which would go great with your twirly plaid skirt, Allie –'

She said this as we stepped on to the playground, which was soggy from last night's rain. As our feet sunk into the inch-deep mud, we noticed a car pull up to the sidewalk next to the school. The passenger-side door opened, and Cheyenne O'Malley, the newest girl in our class (she's here from Canada while her dad is on sabbatical), popped out, wearing a bright pink raincoat and holding a matching pink umbrella, in case it rained later. She closed the car door behind her and, as she went by us on her way to meet her friends Marianne and Dominique, who were waiting for her over by the swings, she put her right foot, in a rain boot with pink hearts printed on it, down in a big puddle on the sidewalk, splashing water all over us.

On purpose.

'Oops!' Cheyenne said, laughing as we looked down at the dirty water stains all over us. 'Sorry! I guess that's what happens when your parents make you walk to school instead of giving you a ride though.'

Then she ran over to 'M and D' (which is what Cheyenne calls Marianne and Dominique), who let out screams of laughter at the hilarious trick she'd played on us. Cheyenne screamed politely back. Then they started talking about what happened last night on *America's Next Top Survivor* or whatever.

'You know, Allie,' Sophie said thoughtfully as she tried to rub the dirty puddle stain out of her coat, 'having a mom who is on TV is only going to boost your popularity at Pine Heights Elementary. No one else has a parent who is a celebrity. Not even Cheyenne, and she's the most popular girl in the whole school.'

'Cheyenne's not the most popular girl in the school,' Caroline pointed out. 'She's just the loudest.'

'*Popularity isn't important*,' I said. '*Being a kind and thoughtful person is.*' That's a rule.

'True,' Sophie said. 'But it can't hurt, is all I'm saying. When is your mom's first show going to be on?'

'Um,' I said, 'Thursday night, I think. So people can tell what movies to go see for the weekend.'

'Perfect,' Sophie said. 'So by Friday morning you'll be the most popular girl around here.'

'Do you really think so?'

Not that being popular was important of course.

But suddenly I thought of how cool it would be to show up to school a different way instead of squishing through the mud with my little brother's hand all hot and sticky in mine. What if Erica and Sophie and Caro-line and I showed up to school in a pure-white stretch limo instead of walking? What would Cheyenne and 'M and D' say if they saw *that*?

If you asked me, this really would be better than aliens showing up and whisking me off to live on a planet where I got a winged unicorn as a pet and everything was made out of candy.

But was it really going to happen?

I guess I was going to have to wait to find out.

Rule #2

There's No Kissing
in Fourth Grade

Mrs Hunter, our fourth-grade teacher, who happens to be the prettiest teacher I have ever met and who could totally have her own TV show if she wanted one, said she had an announcement to make.

I was pretty sure the announcement was going to be about my mom getting the job as film reviewer on *Good News!* I wasn't certain how Mrs Hunter would have found out about it. Maybe she'd ordered a pizza from Pizza Express and Uncle Jay had told her. I'd asked Uncle Jay once if he'd ever delivered a pizza to Mrs Hunter (because I wanted to know if she lived in a house or an apartment, and if she lived in an apartment did it have an elevator) and he said he hadn't.

But you never knew.

Anyway, we all sat very silently in our seats waiting for the announcement, because Mrs Hunter, even as pretty as she was with her nice eye make-up and her high-heeled boots, could be very scary when she wanted to be.

I was totally hoping the announcement would be about my mom, because that would make Cheyenne sorry for what she'd done out in the playground. I could just picture how badly Cheyenne would want to come over to my house once she found out my mom was a TV star. Not that I'd ever let Cheyenne come over to my house. Not after the way she'd treated me and my friends. Cheyenne didn't like to play fun games like Super Spy (pretending to be a spy by seeing how quietly you could walk around the house and spy on the people in it without getting caught) and Science Experiment (mixing up all the different cleansers you find under the bathroom sink to see how many it took before you could make an explosion).

Cheyenne only liked to call boys and ask them if they liked her. *Cheyenne is officially boring*. That's a rule.

Still. It would be very satisfying to say, 'I don't think so,' when Cheyenne begged to come home for lunch with me (Cheyenne thought going home for lunch was the height of dorkiness and that getting a hot lunch, like she and Marianne and Dominique did, was the epitome of cool).

What I *didn't* want the announcement to be was that Mrs Hunter was going away on vacation and that we were going to have a substitute teacher. Mrs Hunter had made an announcement like that once before and it hadn't worked out so well. At least, not when the substitute, Mr White, showed up, since some of the boys in the class had decided it would be a good idea to change seats for the week and pretend to be each other. Stuart Maxwell had given Rosemary and me five boxes of Nerds each in exchange for not telling.

'Children,' Mrs Hunter said as we all sat dreading the return of Mr White. (It's embarrassing to watch a grown man cry.) 'It's the time of year when all the classes begin preparing for the presentation they're going to put on for the Pine Heights Elementary School open house. That's when we invite your parents here to school one evening and put on a little performance to show them what we've been learning this semester. Each grade gets a separate night, and each class within that grade does something different. Mrs Danielson's class, for instance, is going to put on a presentation about early US settlers to this area, which, as you know, we've been studying recently.'

I nearly threw up when I heard this. Not because I was nervous about putting on a presentation. But because putting on a presentation about early US settlers sounded so boring. No offence, but if I had been an early US settler, I'd have gone back to where I came from. First of all, you had to go to the toilet in an *outhouse*. That is a toilet that is *outside* the house, if you know what I mean.

And all the grades in the whole school were in one room! Which would have meant I'd have had to have been in the same room as my little brothers *all day*.

It's bad enough having to live in the same house with my brothers outside school! I'm not spending all day at school in the same room with them too.

I was getting a very bad feeling about what we were going to have to do for our presentation. Because I did not want to have to put on some old-fashioned clothes and stand up and give a speech about walking nine miles to get to the store. No thanks.

Then Mrs Hunter said, 'I thought since all of you have shown so much creativity this year in your essays and drawings on the issue of the environment and what we can do at home to think green, we might do something a little different from the other classes.'

I leaned across my desk to look over at Rosemary, who sits down the row from me, separated only by Stuart Maxwell. Rosemary hunched over her desk to grin at me. I could tell she'd been thinking the same thing about the one-room schoolhouse. Rosemary had

had even more reason than me to be afraid of the US-settler thing. She hates wearing dresses more than any girl in our class. And if we'd had to dress up in old-fashioned clothes, Rosemary would almost certainly have had to wear a skirt . . . a long one. That would have just about killed her.

'For our presentation,' Mrs Hunter went on from the stool where she always sits when she reads to us from Madeleine L'Engle (although now she'd moved on to *The Hobbit*, which wasn't nearly as good, because so far there are no girl characters in it, although sometimes I pretended Bilbo Baggins was a girl, and his real name was Jill, as in *Jildo*), 'I was thinking it would be nice for us to put on a play.'

Everyone in class gasped. Then started chattering excitedly. You could tell right away that the whole class thought the idea of putting on a play was a really, really good one. A much better idea than Mrs Danielson's idea about giving a presentation on US settlers.

I was excited too. I had never been in a play before. Well, except for a little baby play in the first grade in which I played the letter A, because my name started with the letter A. But that didn't count. This would be a proper play, I was sure, in which I would have more lines than *A is for apple . . . and for Allie!*

And hopefully I wouldn't trip over my own feet as I came on to the stage, like I did in first grade, either.

'Oooh, Mrs Hunter,' Cheyenne cried, throwing her hand into the air, eagerly begging to be called on, as always. Rosemary called Cheyenne a suck-up, a word she'd learned from her older brothers. 'Mrs Hunter!'

Mrs Hunter looked over at Cheyenne. 'Yes, Cheyenne?' she asked.

Cheyenne put her arm down. 'May I suggest *Romeo and Juliet* as the play we put on as a class?' she said. 'It is a very moving drama written by a man named William Shakespeare about two teenagers who, even though they are very deeply in love, are kept cruelly apart by their families.'

As Cheyenne said this, she turned her head a little and looked at Patrick Day, who was sitting next to Rosemary in the last row, drawing a picture of James Bond's car with a periscope coming out of the roof, racing stripes down its sides, and fire coming out of the exhaust pipe.

Rosemary and I exchanged horrified glances, and I saw Stuart Maxwell, who was sitting next to me, make a face, while on my other side, Joey Fields squirmed excitedly. I think he was the only person in the whole class, besides Cheyenne and 'M and D', who liked Cheyenne's idea. Everyone else was totally disgusted.

Shakespeare? *Romeo and Juliet*? I'm not positive, but I'm pretty sure there's kissing in that.

The thing is, a while ago, Mrs Hunter had made a rule that *There's no kissing in fourth grade*. Also, no 'going with' people, or any kind of boyfriend/girlfriend stuff.

The only person who'd been upset about that had been Cheyenne (and Joey Fields, who I think sort of secretly dreams about some day having a girlfriend).

Now I could tell Cheyenne was trying to find a way to get round Mrs Hunter's rule by having us all put on a play with kissing in it. No doubt she wanted to play Juliet . . .

. . . and she probably wanted Patrick Day, the boy she wanted to run off to the Brooklyn Bridge with when she turned sixteen, to play Romeo.

Ew!

I could tell the same thought had occurred to Rosemary, since she had wrapped her hands around her own neck and was pretending to strangle herself, with her tongue sticking out. It was kind of hard not to laugh. I mean, it's not like Patrick Day is as cute as Sophie's crush, Prince Peter, or anything. I have actually seen Patrick pick his nose. And eat it.

'Thank you for that suggestion, Cheyenne,' Mrs Hunter said, and for a minute I was worried she was actually considering it. Then she added, 'But I'm not sure we're ready for the Bard just yet.'

Cheyenne looked super disappointed. I guessed from her expression that the Bard must be *Romeo and Juliet* and felt super happy. Yay! We weren't doing Cheyenne's play!

'Instead,' Mrs Hunter went on, 'I took the liberty of writing my own play . . . one with a part for every single person in this class. Allie, would you mind passing out the scripts you'll find on my desk?'

I got up and went to Mrs Hunter's desk (I sit in the last row with all the worst boys in our class – with Rosemary to help me manage them. Our desks are right next to Mrs Hunter's desk, so Mrs Hunter can help supervise the bad boys. So Rosemary and I end up passing things out all the time. It's completely routine for us).

'The play is called *Princess Penelope in the Realm of Recycling*,' Mrs Hunter explained (which I could already tell because I was reading the title as I passed out the scripts). 'It's about a princess named Penelope who runs away from her father's castle after he dies and she learns that her stepmother, the evil queen, is going to try to kill her so the stepmother can inherit the throne instead of Penelope. While trying to reach the home of her beloved fairy godmother, with whom

Penelope knows she'll be safe, she wanders through a strange and wonderful land, the Realm of Recycling. There she meets many strange creatures, such as compact-fluorescent-bulb fairies, public-transportation elves, recycled-paper dragons, water-conservation mermaids, unplug-when-not-in-use unicorns and reusable-water-bottle wizards, who teach Penelope all about ways she can help save the environment so that her father's kingdom, which has begun to be destroyed by pollution and her step-mother's wasteful habits, will be able to be enjoyed by many future generations to come. The creatures of the Realm of Recycling then help Penelope escape from the evil soldiers her stepmother sends to kill her.'

Wow! This play sounded way better than *Romeo and Juliet*. Elves and dragons? Fairies and wizards? And a princess? I totally wanted to be in this play. It sounded fantastic! I couldn't believe Mrs Hunter had written it. It seemed like something a professional writer would have come up with.

And I could tell the rest of the class was excited about it too, if the way people snatched the scripts out of my hands as I passed them out was any indication. Not just the girls either. The boys too.

'Of course,' Mrs Hunter went on in a warning voice as if she could feel the tremor of delight that was going through Room 209, 'this isn't going to be an easy play to put on. There are a lot of lines that will have to be memorized, and a set that will have to be built, and costumes to make, and stage lighting to design, and . . . well, it's going to take all of us pulling together if we're going to make this work. We'll be spending all our art and music classes from now until the open house working on *Princess Penelope in the Realm of Recycling*.'

Cheyenne raised her hand again. She had a copy of Mrs Hunter's script in front of her, because I'd already passed them out to her row.

'Oooh, Mrs Hunter,' Cheyenne said, 'Mrs Hunter!'

Mrs Hunter looked over at her. 'Yes, Cheyenne?' she said in a tired sort of voice.

'Mrs Hunter,' Cheyenne said, putting her hand down, 'I just want to say, on behalf of the class, that I think this play sounds really, really good. And I would like to volunteer to play the part of Princess Penelope.'

The minute she said the words *Princess Penelope*, about half a dozen other hands went flying up into the air . . . all belonging to other girls in Room 209. Every single girl whose hand was up wore an expression that showed she felt outraged over what Cheyenne had just done.

All the girls in our class practically wanted to play the part of Princess Penelope.

'Girls,' Mrs Hunter said, 'put your hands down. You'll all get the chance to audition for the parts you want. That's why Allie is handing out the scripts now. I want you to take them home and give them a read-through tonight. Figure out which parts you'd like to try out for, and then I'll hold auditions tomorrow and make the announcement of who got what part on Friday. We'll start rehearsals on Monday.'

Well! This was a much better way to do it than just giving the part to whoever asked for it first. Everyone had to try out, and whoever did the best job got the part. Kind of like the way my mom had gotten the job of film reviewer for *Good News!*

Except that she'd been the only person who'd applied. At least according to her.

After I'd finished passing out all the scripts, I went back to my desk and picked up the one I'd set down for myself. Mrs Hunter was still talking about the play, but I wasn't paying attention any more. I was too busy reading.

Wow. Princess Penelope had a lot of lines. As I read through them, I could sort of see that Princess Penel-ope was the star of the play.

Well . . . her name *was* in the title.

Hmmm. It would be kind of cool to play a princess

in the class play. Especially if it was the main part. I mean, it would be a lot of lines to memorize.

But think how proud my parents would be when they showed up at the open house to watch *Princess Penelope in the Realm of Recycling* and I was Penelope! *Good News!* might even have me on their show as a guest to talk about my performance – I'm the daughter of one of their stars, after all.

Even better . . . I wouldn't have to work too hard on my costume, because I already had a princess gown: the flower-girl dress I'd worn for my Aunt Mary's wedding last summer (if it still fitted). It would be perfect! It was a long dress made out of shiny gold fabric (Aunt Mary got married in a fancy restaurant at night). It totally looked like something a princess would wear (if I got my mom to do my hair in a bun or braids wrapped around my head).

The problem was, I wasn't the only girl in my class who wanted to play Princess Penelope.

But whatever. I'd figure out a solution to that problem when the time came.

In the meantime, figuring out how I was going to beat Cheyenne for the part we both wanted? That was going to be a pleasure.

Rule #3

It's Rude to Tell Someone
They're Only Going to Get
Something Because No One Else
Wants It, Not Because They
Earned It

I was so busy poring over my copy of the script, I
didn't even hear the bell for recess ring. So I didn't
have any idea what was going on until I noticed
Caroline, Sophie, Erica and Rosemary all standing
around my desk, holding their coats.

'Oh,' I said, looking up. 'Hey, you guys.'

'Aren't you coming outside?' Erica wanted to
know.

'Yeah,' Rosemary said. 'Are you just going to sit
there all day?'

'Huh?' I said, embarrassed I'd been so absorbed
in what I'd been doing. 'Sorry. I guess I didn't hear
the bell.'

'I guess not,' Sophie said with a laugh. 'You must really like that play.'

But I noticed she was still holding her copy of Mrs Hunter's script as well. Even though we were supposed to be going outside to play.

'I do,' I said, getting up and going over to the coat-rack. 'It seems really good. Right? I mean, did you get a chance to read it?'

'I did,' Caroline said. Caroline is one of the fastest readers in our class. She read each of the Harry Potter books in a day. Even the really long ones. 'It's good.'

'What part do you think you're going to try out for?' I asked as I put my coat on.

'I'm going to try for the fairy godmother of reusable-cloth shopping bags,' Erica said. 'Because I've always wanted to be one. A fairy godmother, I mean.'

I wasn't actually surprised to hear this. I mean, Erica loves doing nice things for people. She's always breaking up arguments and telling everyone how nice they look, even when they look awful (that's actually one of my rules: *You should always tell people they look nice, even when they don't. This makes people feel good, so they'll like you better.* Erica is very good at this rule).

'You'd be really good as the fairy godmother,' I said to Erica.

'Wouldn't she?' Sophie said. 'That's what I told her! But she doesn't think she's going to get the part.'

'Oh, I'm not a good enough actress,' Erica said. 'I tried out for *The Sound of Music* when they did it in the community theatre last year, and my sister Missy made it to callbacks, but I didn't.'

'You'll get it,' I told her. 'I just know you will.' I couldn't imagine anyone else in our class getting the part of the fairy godmother. Mostly because I couldn't imagine anyone else *wanting* that part. I mean, who else would want to play the fairy godmother when they could be a princess?

But I didn't say that out loud, because *It's rude to tell someone they're only going to get something because no one else wants it, not because they earned it* (that's a rule).

'Oh,' Erica said, her eyes filling up with tears of gratitude, 'thanks, Allie!' She reached out and gave me a hug. I hugged her back.

See? Just like I said. Total fairy godmother. Or godmother, anyway.

'I want to play one of those evil soldiers,' Rosemary said, her dark eyes flashing with relish. 'Maybe I'll get to carry a sword! And kill Princess Penelope for trying to escape the Castle of Plastic Doom.'

'Princess Penelope doesn't die at the end,' Caroline

said, as we went down the stairs to the playground. 'The evil queen does.'

'Oh.' Rosemary looked disappointed. 'Well, I still want to play an evil soldier. Maybe I can stab Patrick. What about you, Caroline?'

'I've never really been interested in acting,' Caroline said, to my surprise. 'I'll maybe try out for an unplug-when-not-in-use unicorn or something, if we have to be in it. But I'm more interested in running the lights or set design or something.'

I was shocked. I couldn't imagine *anyone* not wanting to be in a play. Who wouldn't want to be up on stage, wearing a costume, pretending to be someone else in front of everyone? That seemed insane to me. The only thing better, if you asked me, would be to be a veterinarian, and save baby animals.

Then again, Caroline is a very practical kind of girl. And acting isn't the most practical kind of thing.

'Who do you want to try out to be, Sophie?' Caroline asked.

To my surprise, Sophie looked shy.

'Oh,' she said, 'I don't know . . .'

'You do so know,' Rosemary said. 'Spill it.'

'No,' Sophie said, 'I don't have any idea. Really. There are so many great parts, it seems like.'

Which was when it hit me:

Oh no! Sophie wanted the role of Princess Penelope!

Of course! That's why she was acting so shy . . . she didn't want to admit it, because she was too modest to say she thought she was a good enough actress to get the lead role.

But that's exactly what she was thinking . . . the same as me!

I don't know how I knew. But I knew, all right. Because I wanted the exact same role.

'Oh my gosh, Sophie,' Erica said. We were outside by then. The sun had finally come out and was drying up the mud puddles. 'You just have to try out for Princess Penelope!'

'That's right, Sophie,' Caroline said. 'If anyone could beat out Cheyenne for that part, it's you . . .'

What? I couldn't believe Caroline had just said that. What about *me*? Couldn't *I* beat out Cheyenne for the part?

'. . . I mean, everyone knows you're the prettiest girl in our whole school,' Caroline went on.

'Oh now,' Sophie said, looking embarrassed. 'Not the whole *school* . . .'

'Well, at least in our grade,' Caroline said. 'Right, Allie?'

The truth was, I had to agree. With her dark curly

hair and big brown eyes, Sophie was extraordinarily beautiful. She may not have looked like a traditional golden-haired storybook princess, but then neither did Cheyenne, since she had dark hair too (Cheyenne just *acted* like a traditional storybook princess, always brushing her long hair at recess, over and over again, and putting it into various sparkle clips).

But Sophie looked like *some* kind of princess anyway. When we played queens at recess, Sophie was always the queen the evil warlord was in love with, because it was so easy to picture someone falling in love with Sophie. She was just that beautiful.

'Yeah,' I said grudgingly. I mean, as much as I wanted to play Princess Penelope myself, I had to admit, Sophie did look more like a princess than I did. If looks were what Mrs Hunter was going for, Sophie was definitely going to get the part over me. Besides, I liked Sophie. I didn't want to hurt her feelings or anything. 'Yeah, Sophie. You should try out for Penelope. You do really look like a princess.'

'And you're kind,' Erica said to Sophie, 'and sweet like a princess too.'

'And intelligent,' Caroline said, 'like a princess is. Way more than Cheyenne.'

'Oh, you guys!' Sophie said, laughing. 'Stop it! You guys are too nice to me!'

The thing was, all those things Caroline and Erica had said were true. Sophie *was* beautiful, kind, sweet and intelligent.

But.

But what about *me*? I mean, I know I don't necessarily *look* like a princess. I'm not as beautiful as Sophie, or as kind or as sweet.

But I'm just as intelligent – maybe more so! I did way better than her in the spelling bee! And I get better grades than Sophie in maths and science!

Plus I'm a very good actress. At least, I think I am. True, I only had that one line in first grade.

But everyone thinks my death scenes during queens are very realistic.

And yet no one had mentioned *me* trying out for Princess Penelope! What was going on?

'You've just got to audition for Princess Penelope, Sophie,' Caroline said. 'Otherwise Cheyenne will get it. And she'll drive us all even more nuts.'

'Yeah,' Rosemary said. 'No way am I putting up with Her Royal Brattiness.'

'Well,' Sophie said, tucking some of her curly hair behind her ear, 'maybe I will.'

'What about you, Allie?' Rosemary asked. 'What part are you going to audition for?'

But of course I couldn't say I wanted to try out for

the part of Princess Penelope. Not now, when everyone had been going on about how fantastic they thought Sophie would be in that role. Because that would seem like I was bragging that I was just as pretty as Sophie or something. Which everyone knew I wasn't. Most of all me.

So I just shrugged and said, 'Oh, I don't know. Maybe I'll go out for the part of one of the creatures who live in the Realm of Recycling or whatever.'

'I thought you were excited about the play,' Caroline said.

Um, why would I be, when all my friends had basic-ally just declared that the only girl in the whole school pretty enough to play the part I wanted was Sophie? Not that I didn't love Sophie – because I totally did – but it might be nice if people would just give me a chance to audition for the part before they all decided Sophie was so perfect for it.

But of course I couldn't say any of that either.

'Oh, I'm excited,' I said instead. 'I just haven't had a chance to read the whole thing yet. I'll look it over and find a role for me. I'll know which one I want by tryouts tomorrow.'

Except of course I knew that by tryouts tomorrow, nothing was going to have changed. I was still going to want to play Princess Penelope, the part Sophie wanted . . . and the part everyone thought she was so perfect for.

And if I auditioned for that role too, everyone was going to be mad at me, for trying to steal Sophie's part.

What was I going to do?

Rule #4

Whenever Possible, Try to Be
Born into a Family with No
Little Brothers

Even though I read through the entire script of *Princess Penelope in the Realm of Recycling* when I got home from school that day (after ballet), I couldn't find a single character in it that I liked better than Princess Penelope.

Oh, there were other parts for girls. There was a fairy queen (she was the leader of the fairies who lived in the Realm of Recycling. The fairy queen teaches Penelope how much better it is to use compact fluorescent bulbs over regular bulbs, because they last longer and use less energy. Then she helps Penelope find her way to her godmother's house).

And there were a couple of mermaids who teach Penelope the importance of water conservation, like taking shorter showers and turning off the water while you brush your teeth.

And then there were some girl elves, who teach Penelope how she should always walk, bike, carpool or take public transportation instead of using a car, since that will lessen her carbon footprint. And a unicorn who advises Penelope to unplug appliances when they aren't in use, as this will save energy as well.

And then of course there was Penelope's fairy godmother and her horrible evil stepmother, the queen, who lives in a plastic castle and doesn't believe in recycling, and just wastes valuable resources and litters every chance she gets because she believes the scientists are wrong about global warming and that we don't need to save our environment for the next generation (and since she's going to kill Penelope anyway I guess her reasoning kind of makes sense).

But why would I want to play a fairy or an elf when I could be Penelope, who was so important that her name was in *the title of the play*?

On the other hand . . . I didn't want to make everyone angry with me. I had said I was going to audition for some other part. So I couldn't just go try out for the part Sophie wanted.

Could I? I mean, wouldn't that be wrong?

I was sitting in my favourite reading spot after dinner – on my window seat, with Mewsie curled up next to me – trying to decide what to do, when the door to my room suddenly burst open.

At first I thought it was the aliens, who'd come to tell me my ride to Planet Voltron was ready.

But it turned out it was just Uncle Jay playing tackle football in the hallway with my brother Mark (even though Mom said *Don't play tackle football in the hallway* outside the kids' rooms any more. That's a rule). He had dived for a pass and crashed into my door, causing it to fly open.

The loud noise made Mewsie spring to his feet, all his long fur rising up to stand on end, so that he looked like a little grey and black striped ball of hair with legs as he stalked around, hissing angrily.

He didn't mean it though. He calmed down right away as soon as he saw who it was.

I didn't calm down right away. I was really mad.

'Stop it,' I yelled when Uncle Jay went rolling all over my floor, with Mark chasing after him, trying to grab the ball away. 'You know you two aren't supposed to be doing that up here!'

'Well, well, well,' Uncle Jay said. He lay collapsed beneath Mark, who had both hands on the ball, trying to prise it out from Uncle Jay's fingers. 'What's eating you?'

'What's eating me is that I would like to have some

privacy once in a while,' I said, stepping over them just as Kevin appeared in the doorway to see what all the commotion was about (he'd been in his room practising the song 'It's the Hard-knock Life' from the musical *Annie*, which he didn't even need to know for the open house. The kindergarteners were just singing a song about rainbows. Kevin sings so loud you can hear him all over the house. His main regret in life, beside not having velvet pants, is that he can't be in *Annie* because he's a boy and there are no boy orphans in *Annie*).

'What's going on in there?' Kevin wanted to know.

'Nothing,' I yelled, and slammed the door closed. Not in his face exactly. But almost.

'Hey,' Kevin yelled from behind the closed door. 'I'm gonna tell. You aren't supposed to *slam doors in people's faces*! That's a rule!'

'Well, I'm gonna tell on these guys,' I yelled back. 'They aren't supposed to play sports up here!'

'No one is going to tell on anyone,' Uncle Jay said, handing the ball to Mark and getting up. 'Because your parents aren't home. They went to that movie your mom has to review. So I'm in charge.'

Uncle Jay opened my door and revealed Kevin on the other side, looking upset because he wasn't in on the action.

'Now, Allie,' Uncle Jay said, turning around to face me, 'what's really wrong?'

'Nothing,' I yelled. 'I just want some privacy, like I said!'

Instead of giving me some privacy, Uncle Jay walked over to the window seat where I'd left Mrs Hunter's script lying face-down. He picked it up and started to read it.

'Oh, sweet,' he said. 'A play. Are you in this, Allie?'

'Not yet,' Kevin said, coming into my room to look over Uncle Jay's shoulder at the script even though

a) I hadn't given him permission to, and

b) he can barely read, being a kindergartener.

'She has to audition,' Kevin explained. 'It's the play her class is putting on for open house. I heard her and her friends talking about it as they walked me home from school.'

Seriously. I have *no* privacy whatsoever.

Whenever possible, try to be born into a family with no little brothers. That's a new rule I just made up.

'This is great,' Uncle Jay said, flipping through the pages of the script. 'What part are you going to audition for, Allie?'

I sank down on to the window seat beside him. I had

pretty much given up on the idea of ever getting any privacy.

'Well,' I said, 'I want to audition for the part of Princess Penelope. But the problem is, one of my best friends is going for that part. And I'm afraid if I try for it too she'll be mad at me. And so will all my other friends.'

Uncle Jay kept flipping through the script. 'Why would they be mad at you?' he wanted to know. 'When I was a drama major, we all lived by the rule that everyone could try for the part he or she wanted, and *May the best man – or woman – win*.'

I had never thought of it that way. It sounded so . . . simple. And like a really great rule.

'I don't know,' I said. 'I still think if I did that they might be mad at me. Because Sophie . . . well, she really wants the part. And besides, she just *looks* like a princess. And I don't.'

'You can say that again,' Mark said. I leaned over to punch him in the arm, but Mark ducked just in time, so my fist just hit air. Mark laughed.

'Who amongst us can say how a princess is sup-posed to look?' Uncle Jay asked, ignoring our fighting. 'There've been many princesses from all over the world – Africa, Japan, Thailand, Hawaii – and I'm sure they haven't looked how we consider traditional princesses should look in the West. But does that make them any less royal? And besides, I'm sure your teacher, who I assume is directing this fine dramatic piece, has her own vision for how her characters should look. How do we know she wasn't picturing you when she wrote the character of Penelope?'

I stared at him, feeling slightly less depressed about the whole thing. 'Do you really think she might have been?' That would be incredible. The truth is, Mrs Hunter once told my grandma I was a joy to have in the classroom. That was a *little* like being a princess. Sort of.

'All I'm saying,' Uncle Jay replied, 'is that we don't know. And neither do your friends. So you might as well try out for the role if you really want to, because otherwise a part of you will always wonder, Could I have been Princess Penelope, if only I had tried? And you don't want to go through life wondering what might have been, do you?'

'No,' I said, shaking my head. That would be terrible. But not as terrible as Sophie and those guys being mad at me.

'And how do you even know your friend is going to get the part?' Uncle Jay asked. 'Some other girl might get it – not you or your friend.'

I sucked in my breath.

41

'Cheyenne O'Malley wants to try for it too!' I cried. 'And if she got it, it would be awful! We all hate her!'

'*It's wrong to hate people,*' Mark said automatically. But only because he'd heard it on TV, not because he actually knows Cheyenne O'Malley.

'So the fact is,' Uncle Jay said, 'some other girl could get the part, some girl you don't even particularly like. Wouldn't your friend be happier if you got the part rather than some girl you didn't like?'

I had never even thought of that, but Uncle Jay was totally right! I mean, what if Mrs Hunter ended up giving the part of Princess Penelope to Cheyenne? How would Sophie and those guys feel then?

And it could totally happen! Because clearly Cheyenne wanted the part, just as badly as Sophie and I did.

'You should totally try out for Princess Penelope, Allie,' Kevin said to me. 'I'm sure Sophie will forgive you.' Then he added thoughtfully, 'Some day.'

'Yeah,' Mark said. 'And since you're probably not going to get it anyway, who even cares?'

'Hey,' Uncle Jay said disapprovingly. 'Let's not be unsupportive of one another's dreams, OK? If we aren't there for each other, who else will be?'

'Yeah,' I said, giving each of my brothers a dirty a look.

'I have an idea,' Uncle Jay said. 'Let's show our support for Allie by helping her practise for her audition.'

'OK! How will we do that?' Kevin wanted to know.

'We'll take turns reading all the other lines, while Allie reads Princess Penelope's dialogue,' Uncle Jay said. 'That way she'll be prepared for the audition tomorrow. Because she'll have an idea how the lines she says should sound.'

'I'd rather play indoor football,' Mark grumbled.

'Just for that you get to be the evil queen,' Uncle Jay said, hitting Mark on the top of his head with the rolled up script.

So we spent the next hour doing what Uncle Jay had suggested. He and Mark read all the other lines in the play, while I read all Princess Penelope's. Occasionally Uncle Jay let Kevin 'read' a line (meaning that Uncle Jay whispered the line into Kevin's ear and Kevin said it aloud with great dramatic flair).

'Americans used fifty billion plastic water bottles last year,' Kevin read out loud (or repeated what Uncle Jay whispered to him). 'Seventy-six per cent of which were not recycled. It will take over one thousand years for them to decompose!'

'Oh no, Reusable-water-bottle Wizard,' I cried. 'I had no idea!'

'Yes,' Kevin said. 'That's why you should reuse your water bottles, or better still, just drink out of a glass!'

By the time we'd finished the whole play, I felt like I had a real grasp for Princess Penelope's character . . . like I knew what made her tick, as Uncle Jay put it. He said it was important for any thespian (which means actor or actress) who knows her craft to have such a feel for her character that she could tell the director what kind of cereal that character had for breakfast.

I decided that Princess Penelope would eat Count Chocula, because she's a princess and can have whatever kind of cereal she wants (we aren't allowed to have sugary cereals in our house because Mom says sugar makes us hyper).

We'd finished the play and were getting ready for bed when I asked Uncle Jay why, if he knew so much about acting, he'd decided not to stay a theatre major.

'Oh, that's easy,' he said. 'Because as a career, it's totally cut-throat. I prefer the gentler climes of creative writing. And now, because I don't have rehearsals, I have my evenings free to hang out with you guys.'

Awww!

As I drifted off to sleep that night, I couldn't help feeling like I was way better prepared for the audition than either Sophie or Cheyenne. I mean, I had rehearsed the part I wanted with a semi-professional actor! Or at least a former theatre major. I highly doubted the two of them had done the same.

And even if they had, had he given them such good advice, such as, Figure out what your character ate for breakfast?

Probably not.

I was going to be the best Princess Penelope Mrs Hunter had ever seen. And if my getting the part hurt Sophie's feelings, well, that would be OK. She'd get over it, just like Uncle Jay had said.

Probably.

Rule #5

May the Best Man –
Or Woman – Win

My mom was in a bad mood at breakfast the next morning. She said it was because *Requiem for a Somnambulist* had turned out not to be a very good movie.

'The name of the show is *Good News!*,' she said worriedly. 'I just don't want my first review to be a negative one.'

'The *good news* is that you'll be saving people from having to go see that snooze-fest,' said Dad. 'In fact, that's what you should call it in your review. A snooze-fest. I know it put me to sleep.'

'And you were snoring,' Mom said. 'That's the last time I'm taking you to see any of the films I'm assigned to review.'

'Oh, I'm really sad to hear that,' Dad said, not sounding sad at all.

I wasn't in the best of moods either, but not because

of *Requiem for a Somnambulist* being bad. I was nervous about my audition. Now that I was actually about to face them, I wasn't so confident any more about how my friends were going to act when they found out I was auditioning for the part of Princess Penelope. It was one thing to tell yourself you were going to do something at night before you fell asleep.

It was another thing to wake up the next morning and actually go about doing it.

I had to tell Kevin and Mark not to say anything to Erica when she came to the door. About me wanting to play Princess Penelope, I mean. I said I was going to tell her and Caroline and Sophie in my own time.

Mark told me he wouldn't say anything if I gave him my dessert at lunch, which was totally unfair since I hadn't told on him about the football-in-the-house thing . . . but I agreed. Kevin said he wouldn't tell at all, which was nice of him . . . except that I knew he was just saying that so I'd keep on walking him to school, because if I refused, Mom or Dad or Mark would have to walk him, and he wouldn't have nearly as much fun as he does with me, since my friends fight over who gets to hold his hand (for some reason, they find him cute).

Although today, Caroline, Sophie and Erica were all too nervous about the audition to remember to argue over who got the privilege of holding on to Kevin's sweaty fingers. Erica was still reading her script as she came up to our front porch to ring the bell.

'Oh, Allie,' she said, when I got to the door, 'this is going to be harder than I thought it was! The fairy godmother has so many lines! How will I ever remember that plastic bags are all made from polythene, which may take as long as five hundred years to degrade, and only one out of every five plastic bags is ever recycled?'

'You don't have to remember all that today,' I reminded her. 'You can just read from the script during the audition. Mrs Hunter didn't say anything about us having to memorize the part by today.'

'Yes,' Erica said, 'I know. But if I get the part, I'll have to remember them all some day. And how am I going to do that?'

'I know all the songs in *Annie* by heart,' Kevin volunteered as we made our way to the Stop sign, where I could see Sophie and Caroline waiting for us. 'Just because I've sung them so many times.'

'That's right,' I said. '*Practice makes perfect.*' That's a rule.

'Are you ready for the audition?' Erica asked Sophie and Caroline as soon as we'd gotten close enough to speak.

'No. I'm so nervous,' Sophie said. She held out her hand. 'Look at my fingers. They're shaking so much, my mom thought there might be something wrong with me and she wanted to take me to the doctor instead of letting me go to school today.'

It was true. Sophie's fingers *were* shaking a lot. I felt worse than ever about trying out for the part of Penelope.

Then I remembered what Uncle Jay had said – that there was a chance Mrs Hunter might have envisioned me, or even Cheyenne, instead of Sophie, in the role, and there was no guarantee she'd even get the part anyway – and I made myself calm down.

'As long as Cheyenne doesn't get the part,' I said. 'Right?' Everyone agreed.

'Seriously,' Caroline said, 'I can barely put up with her under normal circumstances. But her getting the lead in the class play? And the part of a *princess*? No thanks. Rosemary was right. We have to keep Her Royal Brattiness from getting it!'

'We all have to really try to make sure that doesn't happen,' I said. I didn't mention that I was going to try to make sure that didn't happen by going for the part myself though.

'Totally,' Sophie said.

'Definitely,' Erica said.

'Good idea,' Kevin said even though no one was talking to him.

Mrs Hunter was holding the auditions in the school auditorium during the time we normally had art class. Waiting so long – art class wasn't until after morning recess, during which time we had to endure Cheyenne going on and on about how sure she was that she was going to get the part, because she's had so much experience and has such long hair and is princess-like – was murder.

'The thing is,' Cheyenne was telling everyone at recess, 'back in Canada, I was actually the lead in all my school plays. I played Anne Shirley in our school's production of *Anne of Green Gables*. And Helen Keller in our school's production of *The Miracle Worker*. So I really deserve the part of Princess Penelope. Because I've been the lead in so many plays before. I brought my head shot and résumé in to show Mrs Hunter. I guess none of you brought head shots and résumés, did you?'

'Well,' Caroline said, 'maybe not. But everyone knows Sophie looks the most like a princess out of all the girls in the entire school.'

Cheyenne just glanced over at 'M and D' and started laughing at that.

'Sure she does,' Cheyenne said. 'Anything you say, Caroline.'

Really, I know *It's wrong to hate people*, like Mark said. That's a rule. But it's kind of hard not to hate Cheyenne.

When it was time for the auditions, Mrs Hunter made our class line up. Then she led us down to the auditorium (which is also the gym and the cafeteria. Pine Heights Elementary is way old-fashioned). Once we'd sat down (on the gym floor, where it was sometimes possible to find an old squashed French fry the custodial arts manager, Mr Elkhart, had missed), each kid was allowed to go up on stage and read from the part he or she wanted to play. This made the audition time very short for kids like Stuart Maxwell who just wanted to play one of the evil queen's soldiers. I mean, he just went marching across the stage and said, 'Yes, Your Majesty! The pollution ray is ready!' That was the soldier's only line.

Which was fine with Stuart, because he didn't want to spend time memorizing lines. He just wanted to carry a spear, use it to threaten to kill Princess Penelope, and look cool on the night of our class open house. I know this because Stuart Maxwell told me so himself.

But as it turned out, every single girl in our class,

with the exception of Rosemary, who wanted to play a soldier too (and Erica, who wanted to play the fairy godmother, and Caroline, who wanted to play the unicorn), longed to play Princess Penelope.

We figured that out as we were sitting on the floor, waiting for our turn to go up on stage, and girl after girl went up and read the same part – Princess Penelope's speech to her stepmother about the importance of recycling, and how if we're going to preserve the planet for future generations, we've got to leave it a cleaner place than we found it. After which Princess Penelope nobly gives herself up to save the planet from being destroyed by the evil queen's pollution ray (but the princess's fairy godmother makes everything OK by weaving a spell of protective reusable-cloth shopping bags around Penelope and the Realm of Recycling. Then the evil queen's pollution ray bounces off it and ends up hitting her in the chest and striking her down dead).

Sophie, Caroline, Erica, Rosemary and I sat next to each other during the auditions, and we clapped really loud for each girl as she tried out, even though, to tell the truth, most of them really, really stank.

I don't mean to sound rude, but they just really did.

'She's not putting any *feeling* into it,' Sophie whispered about Marianne's performance.

And it was really true. Marianne was reading off Penelope's lines from the script like a robot.

'Maybe she's just nervous,' Erica, always trying to see the bright side of things, whispered.

'We're *all* nervous,' Sophie whispered.

'I'm not nervous,' Rosemary said.

'She means most of us are nervous,' Caroline whispered. 'But we know not to sound like robots.'

Dominique went next. She didn't sound like a robot, but she wasn't any good either. She read through Princess Penelope's lines so fast, you could hardly understand what she was saying.

'Thank you, Dominique,' Mrs Hunter said.

'That was terrible,' Sophie whispered when Dominique had gotten back to her seat. 'It really was.'

We all had to agree.

'Sophie Abramowitz?' Mrs Hunter said.

It was Sophie's turn.

She let out a little gasp. We each grabbed one of her hands for support and squeezed. Her hands were very sweaty. Then she let go, picked up her script and hurried up on to the stage.

If Sophie was nervous, you couldn't tell by the way she read. She didn't go too fast and she put a lot of feeling into it. She did a totally perfect Penelope. If I was Mrs Hunter, I'd give her the part. Not only did Sophie look pretty, with her curly hair and dark eyes, but she sounded good too. When she begged the evil queen (played by Mrs Hunter, sitting out in the audience) to consider recycling for the good of future generations, you could really hear the sympathy for the fairy folk in her voice.

I only hoped that when it was my turn, I could do as good a job as Sophie.

'Thank you, Sophie,' Mrs Hunter said when she was done.

'That was amazing,' we all said when Sophie got back to her seat.

'Do you really think so?' Sophie asked. 'I was so nervous. I stumbled over a lot of the words.'

'You couldn't tell at all,' Erica said, and for once she wasn't just being nice. You really couldn't tell.

'Cheyenne O'Malley?' Mrs Hunter said, and it was Cheyenne's turn to go up and read.

'Mrs Hunter,' Cheyenne said, stopping in front of Mrs Hunter on her way to the stage, 'I'll be reading for the part of Princess Penelope today. And here's my résumé and head shot.'

We started giggling then. We couldn't help it. A résumé?

'Why, thank you, Cheyenne,' Mrs Hunter said, taking the photo and paper Cheyenne gave her.

Then Cheyenne climbed up on to the stage. 'May I begin?' she asked.

'You may,' Mrs Hunter said.

And Cheyenne began.

We stopped giggling then. Because Cheyenne seemed so professional. Also, we wanted to see how good she was in comparison to Sophie. The truth was, I suspected Cheyenne would be good, because she'd been bragging to everyone about how much she'd practised last night.

But I didn't expect her to be as good as she was. Which was very, very good. If I had thought I could hear Sophie's voice throb with sympathy for the fairy folk, well, Cheyenne was *crying* for the fairy folk. With real tears!

I couldn't believe it. I'd never seen anyone cry on stage like that. Unless, like, a hammer had accidentally fallen on their toe or something.

'Somebody has to bring that girl down,' Rosemary said, 'or when I get the part of the evil soldier, I'm going to kill her for real.'

'Shh,' Sophie said. 'I'm watching.'

'What for?' Rosemary asked. 'She's terrible!'

'No,' Sophie whispered, looking worried. 'She's really, really good!'

I thought Cheyenne was good too. She was so

dramatic, everyone in the whole gym was watching her with his or her mouth hanging open . . . even Patrick Day, who'd snuck in his DS. But for the few minutes while Cheyenne was acting, he didn't seem to care what happened to Super Mario.

It seemed impossible to imagine anyone could act better than Cheyenne O'Malley. Except possibly Miley Cyrus.

When she was done with the scene, Cheyenne curtsied the way a real princess would, then wiped the tears from her cheeks. There was stunned silence for a moment.

Then everyone clapped like crazy.

'Oh my goodness,' Sophie said as she clapped. She wasn't smiling or anything. It was like she didn't want to clap, but she had to. At least, that's how I felt. 'Oh my goodness, I think I'm going to be sick.'

'*You're* going to be sick?' Rosemary said as she clapped. 'How do you think *I* feel? We can't let her get the part.'

'What are we going to do to stop it from happening?' Caroline asked. Her clapping was hiding how disgusted her voice sounded. 'I mean . . . she can cry on cue. I'm surprised she doesn't have her own TV show.'

STAGE FRIGHT

'Allie Finkle?' Mrs Hunter called my name over the sound of everyone's clapping.

I swallowed. Hard.

'Well,' I said, blowing some hair up out of my face, 'I guess it's up to me. I'll have to go for that part too.'

Sophie, Caroline and Erica stared at me as I got up. They'd all stopped clapping.

'Wait,' Sophie said. '*You're* going for the part of Penelope?'

'I guess I have to,' I said. 'We have to beat Cheyenne, right? And the more people who try, the better. Right?' That was the strategy I'd decided to tell them I was going for, in the hopes they'd understand why I was auditioning for the part of Princess Penelope, and not be mad at me. It had sort of occurred to me as Cheyenne had been doing her crying bit.

And the amazing thing was . . . it seemed to work!

'Don't be better than me!' Sophie cried.

'I won't,' I assured her. 'I'll just be better than Cheyenne.' Only I was lying, of course. I fully intended to be better than both of them. If I could.

Did that make me a bad friend? I hoped not! But it was like Uncle Jay said . . . may the best woman win!

'Go, Allie,' Erica said. 'You can do it!'

The walk up to the stage seemed like the longest walk in the world. Why hadn't I noticed how far it was from the gym floor to the stage? On my way there, I passed Cheyenne, coming back to her seat. She made a face at me, a sort of *Go Ahead and Try to Beat Me* face.

Well, guess what? I was going to.

There was just one problem. My fingers were shaking even more than Sophie's had been that morning by the Stop sign. I could barely hold on to the script, my fingers were trembling so hard.

Only . . . what had I got to be so nervous about? I was going to beat Cheyenne, that was all.

And I was going to do it by not making Princess Penelope a big crybaby. I was going to make her be exactly the way I'd rehearsed her last night with Uncle Jay – a cool girl who saves the Realm of Recycling. And who eats Count Chocula for breakfast.

By the time I'd climbed all the way to the stage, walked out into the middle of it and turned to face everyone, I felt like I wasn't Allie Finkle any more. I was Princess Penelope. I was going to fight for my father's throne, for a reduction in carbon emissions and for all the creatures who lived in the Realm of Re-cycling. I'd forgotten all about Cheyenne. Even though I could see her laughing and whispering with her friends.

But that didn't matter. Because I was a princess.

What did I care about a silly fourth-grade girl and her head shot and résumé?

Instead I looked down at Mrs Hunter's script and began to read my lines in a clear, strong voice, making sure to project – not *pro*ject, but pro*ject*, as in pro*ject* my voice, which was something Uncle Jay had told me about. It means making sure your voice carries all the way to the back of the room, so even people in the last row of the theatre can hear you. I was pretty sure I could do it, because I'd never had a problem with being loud before. In fact, I'd had a problem with Mrs Harrington, Erica's mom, asking if I could *lower* my voice a little when we played dollhouse at Erica's house and I got a little too dramatic. I could be even louder than Cheyenne if I wanted to. I could be louder than anyone.

I knew my portrayal of Princess Penelope was working – and that I was projecting all right – because everyone from Room 209 was staring up at me with their mouths hanging open just as hard as they'd been staring up at Cheyenne. Patrick Day had stopped playing Super Mario Bros again, and even Cheyenne and Marianne and Dominique had stopped whispering. I said my lines exactly the way Uncle Jay and I had rehearsed them, giving them a lot of emotion and depth. The only real problem occurred at one point when I thought I heard Mrs Hunter laugh.

But why would she laugh, when the part I was reading was from a totally serious scene of the play? Uncle Jay had not laughed once when I was doing it. And I had done it for him five or six times.

So probably I had misheard her.

When I was done, there was a moment of silence. Then, just like with Cheyenne, everyone started clapping. *Everyone.* Even Lenny Hsu.

And Lenny hates everything. Except dinosaurs.

That's when I discovered something: there is something totally great about hearing people clap for you. It's even better than Count Chocula cereal. It's even better than being called a joy to have in the classroom by your favourite teacher of all time.

I sort of wondered if it would be cooler than saving the lives of little baby animals, the way a veterinarian does.

When I got to where my friends were sitting, Erica was the first one to grab me by the hand.

'Oh my gosh, Allie,' she cried, 'you were so good! I had no idea you were such a good actress!'

'Thanks,' I said letting her pull me down next to her. I was glad she had liked my performance, but I couldn't help looking over at Sophie. She was smiling too, along with Caroline and Rosemary. But there seemed to be a slightly worried expression on her face.

'You were really great,' Caroline said.

'Much better than Cheyenne,' Rosemary said. 'You blew her out of the water.'

'Thanks,' I said, again. 'My Uncle Jay helped me rehearse. It turns out he used to be a theatre major.'

I turned towards Sophie, who I noticed hadn't said anything. I was getting more nervous than ever that she might be mad.

And the only way to handle that, I knew, was to say something about it. *It's always better to have things out in the open than to let them fester*. That's a rule.

'You aren't mad at me for trying out for Princess Penelope, are you, Sophie?' I asked. 'The last thing I want to do is ruin our friendship. But we have to do everything we can to stop Cheyenne getting the part. Anyway, you were so good, I know you're going to get it.'

And *The best way to keep a person from getting mad at you is to compliment them. Even if you don't think it's true*. This is a rule.

It totally worked on Sophie. She smiled, all the worry gone from her face, and said, 'Oh no, Allie, I'm not mad. I understand. You just did it to make Cheyenne's performance look even worse. Which you did. And besides, I'm not going to get the part. You are.'

'No,' I said, 'you are.'

'No,' Sophie said, 'you are.'

'No,' I said, 'you are.'

'No,' she said, 'you are.'

'Would you two cut it out?' Rosemary said, 'You're making me dizzy.'

So it turned out Uncle Jay had gotten it exactly right. Sophie wasn't mad. It really *was* 'May the best man – or woman – win' in the theatre.

And now it was up to Mrs Hunter. All of us hoped she wouldn't give the role of Princess Penelope to Cheyenne. But it was kind of hard to believe she wasn't at least considering it.

'I mean, she brought a head shot and résumé,' Sophie said as we walked home from school that day. 'And she *cried*. She actually cried. Those were real tears. You know, she could make herself sick getting herself worked up that way.'

We agreed. We all remembered the tears. It was kind of hard to forget them. Cheyenne hadn't let us, for one thing. She'd brought them up multiple times throughout the day.

'I learned that technique when I was in *Anne of Green Gables*,' she'd explained during the afternoon to anyone who would listen. 'The director told me to think of the saddest thing that ever happened to me.

So I always think of the time my mom told me she'd take me and all my friends to see the Jonas Brothers in concert for my birthday. But she didn't buy the tickets in time, and they sold out. So I had to take my friends to *Beauty and the Beast on Ice* instead. It was the most embarrassing thing ever. I didn't speak to her for a month. Whenever I think about it, my eyes fill up. See? They're doing it now.'

We looked, and it was true. Cheyenne could make herself cry at will just by thinking about how she'd missed out on seeing the Jonas Brothers in concert on her birthday.

'I should have cried,' Sophie said with a sigh.

'No,' Caroline said. 'You were good! Don't beat yourself up about it.'

'You were the best,' Erica said. Then she quickly corrected herself. 'You and Allie were both the best Penelopes. Totally different, but the best. It will be hard for Mrs Hunter to decide. I'm glad I'm not her!'

Except I didn't think it was going to be hard for Mrs Hunter to decide at all. Because I had something neither Sophie nor Cheyenne had – a mom who was on the show *Good News!* Not that this had anything to do with how well I was going to portray the part of Princess Penelope!

It's just that my mom reviewed things. Such as movies. So why not plays?

And wouldn't Mrs Hunter want her play reviewed on TV?

I wasn't about to point this out to Sophie or Erica or Caroline. I wasn't going to be a braggart about it. It was just a fact. When my mom made her debut that night on *Good News!*, and Mrs Hunter saw it – and I knew she'd be watching, because I'd casually mentioned to her that my mom would be on while we were lining up for recess. Just a, 'Hey, Mrs Hunter. Guess what?' kind of thing – then she might be more inclined to give me the part.

I knew it wasn't exactly fair. But were Sophie's gorgeous brown eyes and hair fair? Had Cheyenne's head shot and résumé been fair? Or her using her tragic Jonas Brothers incident to make herself cry?

There's nothing fair about life on the stage. It's cutthroat, like Uncle Jay had said. *If you want to get anywhere, you can't play by the rules.*

And that's a rule.

Rule #6

Friends Try to Make
Friends Feel Better

In honour of her television debut, my mom was having a little party at our house. To it she had invited Erica's family, including Erica's big sister Missy and older brother John, and my Uncle Jay and his girlfriend Harmony. They all showed up right before dinner, because *Good News!* is on at seven. Dad was serving his championship chilli, along with nachos and a special drink for the adults in a funny glass shaped like a cactus. Us kids got to drink plain old juice.

'To Liz's debut,' the adults kept saying as they clinked their glasses. Then they laughed like crazy.

Harmony was super impressed by Mom's new job. She's studying to be a journalist at the same college where Mom and Dad work and where Uncle Jay goes to. She's a big fan, it turns out, of *Good News!*

'Have you gotten to meet Lynn Martinez?' Harmony asked Mom. Lynn Martinez is the main host of *Good News!*

'Yes,' Mom said. 'She's very nice.'

'I'll bet,' Harmony said. 'Do you think you could get me an internship there with her this summer?'

'Uh,' Mom said, 'maybe. I'll ask.'

'Thanks. It would mean so much,' Harmony said.

'This is so exciting,' Erica kept saying, as we shovelled nachos into our mouths (mine didn't have any salsa on them though, because of my rule about not eating anything red). 'Aren't you excited, Allie?'

'I'm totally excited,' I said. Everyone was excited, except for Erica's sister Missy, who wouldn't stop texting her friends, and her brother John, who was playing indoor football upstairs with Mark (I could tell from all the thumping, although my mom hadn't figured it out yet).

'Aren't you excited, Missy?' Erica asked her sister.

'Yeah,' Missy said, not sounding excited at all. She didn't look up from her cellphone keypad. 'I'm so excited I could just die.'

'She doesn't mean it,' Erica told me apologetically. 'She's really excited. Living next door to you is like living next door to a movie star.'

'I know,' I said. I mean, I didn't want to sound like a braggart. But it was true.

'Hey, everyone, shh, she's on, she's on,' said Mrs Harrington, who was more excited than anyone.

And there was my mom, on TV!

It amazing to see your own mom, someone you've known your whole life, on a famous TV show. She looked so great, and not nervous at all. It was hard to hear what she was saying, because everyone was screaming so loud, but I think mostly she was saying not to go see *Requiem for a Somnambulist*, and why.

'If you're looking for a preachy, pretentious snore-fest of a film on which to waste ten dollars and fifty cents, I could not recommend *Requiem for a Somnambulist* more,' Mom said, smiling into the camera. 'Or you could just save your money and stay home and watch *Good News!* instead.'

The minute she appeared on the TV screen, my real-life mom went, 'Oh no!' and put both hands over her mouth.

'What's wrong, Liz?' Dad asked, laughing. 'You look great.'

'You look fantastic, Elizabeth,' Mrs Harrington said. 'That's a great colour on you.'

'I picked it out for her,' Kevin said all proudly.

But Mom still looked upset. 'They have no budget

for a make-up artist,' she said. 'So I did my own. Lynn kept saying to be sure to use a heavy hand because the lights really wash people out, but I had no idea . . .'

'You look really pretty, Mom,' I said.

But Mom just said, 'Where are my eyelashes? I look like a rabbit.'

'You don't look like a rabbit, Mom,' I said, peering at the TV. In no way did my mom look like a rabbit. Besides, even if she did, wouldn't that be a good thing? Rabbits are cute and cuddly and everyone loves them. Even if they do poop in your hand.

'Ha,' Missy said, looking up from her cellphone keypad. 'You do kind of look like a rabbit, Mrs F.'

John and Mark had come down to the TV room to join us. John started laughing.

'John Junior! Melissa Ann!' Mrs Harrington said. 'Do you want to go home right now?'

'Yes,' Missy said.

'Ignore her, Elizabeth,' Mr Harrington said. 'You looked great. And thanks to you, I'll be telling everyone in my office not to see *Requiem for a Somnambulist* now, based on your advice.'

Uncle Jay brought Mom another special drink. He said, 'Here's to the star!'

Mom drank her special drink in practically one

gulp. 'I think I'm going to step outside for a minute for a breath of fresh air.'

The phone started ringing, so Kevin ran to answer to answer it. 'Hello, this is Kevin Finkle speaking,' he said. All of us kids were *supposed to answer the phone politely* that way (only I said, 'This is Allie Finkle speaking,' and Mark said, 'This is Mark Finkle speaking.' It was a rule).

'Mom,' Kevin yelled after he'd hung up, 'that was Mrs Hauser. She says to tell you she just saw you on TV and you looked really great!'

'Fantastic,' Mom said. Only she didn't sound like she actually thought it was too fantastic.

'Now, Liz,' Dad said. 'You're overreacting.'

'Am I, Tom?' Mom asked him. 'Am I really?'

The phone rang again. Kevin ran to get it. 'This is Kevin Finkle speaking.'

'Allie,' he called after a moment, 'it's Caroline.'

Erica and I ran to the phone.

'Hello?' I said, holding the receiver so Erica could listen in too.

'Oh my gosh, Allie,' Caroline cried. 'We just saw your mom –'

'I'm here too, Allie, I'm over at Caroline's on the extension,' Sophie cried.

'– and she was so funny,' Caroline said.

'And she looked so pretty!' Sophie said.

'She thinks she looked like a rabbit,' I said.

'Why would she think that?' Caroline asked.

'I don't know,' I said. 'She just does.'

'She didn't look anything like a rabbit. She looked totally beautiful,' Sophie said. 'I called my mom and she thought so too. Plus she thought the stuff she said about that movie was hilarious.'

'My dad thought so too,' Caroline said. 'He was laughing. Wasn't he, Sophie?'

'He was,' Sophie said.

'That's good,' I said. 'I'll tell my mom.'

'So, see you at the Stop sign tomorrow?' Caroline said.

'Yeah,' I said.

'I'm so nervous about the play,' Sophie said. 'I'm so nervous I can't eat. My mom is worried I'm giving myself an ulcer. I'm really scared Cheyenne is going to get the part of Princess Penelope.'

'She won't,' Erica said.

'She won't,' I echoed, even though I had no way of knowing that for sure. Still, *Friends try to make friends feel better.* That's a rule. 'She's too big a crybaby.'

'Maybe Princess Penelope is *supposed* to be a crybaby,' Sophie said.

'No,' I said. 'Princesses aren't supposed to cry.

Princesses are strong. They have to be, for the light-bulb fairies and transportation elves they're supposed to protect.'

'Oh,' Sophie said. 'I never thought of that.'

The call waiting went off. 'That's the other line,' I said. 'I have to go.'

'OK,' Caroline said. 'See you tomorrow.'

'See you tomorrow,' I said, and hung up. 'This is Allie Finkle speaking,' I said, to whoever was on the other line.

'Hello, Allie Finkle,' said a lady. 'This is your mother's friend Joyce from work. Is she there? I'd like to tell her what a great job she did on *Good News!* just now.'

'Sure,' I said. 'I'll go get her.'

So. It was starting. Basically, my mom's first TV appearance had only ended *five minutes ago*, and she was already a celebrity! My dramatic life-change was about to begin.

And sure, after everyone went home, my dad made me help him fill the dishwasher.

But I didn't mind because soon, I knew, we'd have a housekeeper to do all that, just like Mary Kay Shiner. Maybe even a butler. I mean, the family of a big TV star couldn't be expected to empty and fill their own dishwasher! That would just be ridiculous.

After this week, I'd probably never have to do a single chore again.

It was really hard to sleep that night. For one thing, Mewsie was still so excited from the party (he loved having company) that he kept bouncing around my room, batting his catnip ball back and forth. It was really, really annoying, but he was still too little to let outside – especially at night.

Plus, I couldn't stop thinking about my new life as the daughter of a TV star. When I got to school, probably the kids were going to swarm all over me and stuff. It was going to be really hard to sign all those autographs without getting a wrist cramp, but I was just going to have to try. I didn't want them to think I was a snob, like Cheyenne!

Then there was the part where I was maybe – probably – going to get the role of Princess Penelope. This would obviously make people even *more* jealous of me. I mean, if it happened. Which it might not. But it probably would. I was going to have to be very sympathetic to Sophie when she started crying because *she* didn't get the part of Princess Penelope.

I wouldn't be at all sympathetic to Cheyenne, though. Because I didn't care about her at all.

Even though I thought I'd never fall asleep, I must have, because I woke up the next morning to find

Mewsie massaging my hair and making tangles out of it, as usual. I carefully removed his claws and got dressed, putting on my best purple leggings and denim skirt, my high-tops and my most colourful hoody. I knew it was important that I looked good for my first day as a TV star's daughter and as the star of my school play . . . but not too good. I didn't want people to think I was a snob.

Because that's what happens when you're a star and all. Most people love you. But some people can't rise above their jealousy. They warn about stuff like that all the time in Missy's teen magazines.

When Erica came to pick me up to walk to school, she didn't seem to notice how carefully I'd picked out my clothes, or the beautiful styling job I'd done on my hair, using many multicoloured sparkle clips.

But that was OK. I realized it was just because I'd been so subtle about it.

And when we got to the Stop sign, Caroline and Sophie didn't notice either. That was OK too.

'Allie,' Caroline said, instead of saying anything about my new look, 'your mom was so good last night.'

'And she looked so pretty,' Sophie said.

'I know,' Erica said. 'Didn't she? I didn't think she looked like a rabbit at all.'

'I wonder how many people saw her,' I said. That wasn't really what I wanted to know though. What I really wanted to know was if Mrs Hunter had seen her and been so impressed by all the fine actresses in my family that she had decided to give me the part of Princess Penelope.

'Probably the whole town saw her,' Erica said.

'Everyone who wasn't watching *Entertainment Tonight*,' Caroline said.

'No one watches that show,' Sophie said scornfully. 'It's boring.'

'Missy watches it,' Erica said. 'She always wants to find out what her favourite teen sensations are up to.'

'Oh well,' Sophie said. 'Missy.' And she rolled her eyes.

We were at the school by then, and Kevin, bursting with the desire to spread the news about our mom to the kindergarten set, dropped Erica and Caroline's hands and went running towards the jungle gym, screaming, 'My mom was on TV last night!'

Cringing with embarrassment, I looked around for somewhere to hide. But it was too late. Some fifth-grade girls, who always keep an eye out for Kevin's arrival to see what extraordinary outfit he might have on, came up to me right away. One of them, who had red hair pulled back in Hello Kitty hairslides, asked, 'What's he talking about?'

'Oh,' I said. This so wasn't happening how I'd pictured it. Where was my long white stretch limo? And where were my bodyguards to protect me from the paparazzi? 'Nothing.'

'It's not nothing,' Sophie said excitedly. 'Her mom is the new film reviewer on *Good News!* She was on last night. She called that new movie *Requiem for a Somnambu*-whatsit a preachy, pretentious snooze-fest.'

The red-haired fifth-grader looked surprised.

'That was your mom?' she said. She called across the playground to another group of fifth-grade girls. 'Hey, Katie! Guess what? The little pirate kid's mom is the new film reviewer for *Good News!*'

The fifth-grader she was calling to stopped texting and ran over to where we were standing. The friends she'd been with put away their cellphones and came running over as well.

'No way,' Katie said to me. 'That was your mom?'

'Yeah,' I said. I couldn't believe all these fifth-graders were actually talking to me. And for once it had nothing to do with my brother showing up to school in a funny costume.

'That's really cool,' a fifth-grade girl in a pair of

jeans with rhinestones on them said. 'What movie is she going to do next?'

'I don't know,' I said. I couldn't believe it was finally happening. I was becoming famous. *And I hadn't even been kidnapped by aliens or cast as Princess Penelope yet!*

'What's going on over here?' someone wanted to know, and we all looked around to see Cheyenne and her friends 'M and D' approaching. Cheyenne looked mad. Why did she look so mad? Had Mrs Hunter told her who'd gotten the part of Princess Penelope already, and it hadn't been her? But how could she? School hadn't even started yet.

'This girl's mom is the new film reviewer on *Good News!*,' the red-haired fifth-grader told Cheyenne, pointing at me.

Cheyenne looked at me and sneered. 'So? I've never even heard of that show.'

Caroline, Sophie, Erica and I all looked at each other. Who had never even heard of *Good News!*? It was like the most famous show in our town ever.

You could tell the fifth-grade girls all felt the same way, since they started laughing. Only not with Cheyenne. At her.

'You've never heard of *Good News!*?' the girl in the

rhinestone jeans said. 'It's only the most popular show in our whole town. What's wrong with you?'

Cheyenne's face turned a funny colour pink. The thing is, the fifth-grade girls are the coolest girls in our school. Getting made fun of by them is the worst. It's almost as bad as getting made fun of by Cheyenne.

'Well,' Cheyenne said, sticking out her pointy chin, 'I'm from Canada. We don't have that show there.'

'Well, you live here now, don't you?' the red-haired fifth-grader asked. 'You better start watching it, if you want to know what's going on.'

With that, the fifth-grade girls turned and walked away.

Meanwhile, Cheyenne's face turned bright red. Because of course she thought she already knew what was going on. Finding out she didn't was quite a surprise to her. It was such a surprise that even her best friends, Marianne and Dominique, giggled at the shock of it.

This caused Cheyenne to twirl around and say, 'Shut up!' to them. Then she stuck out one hip and put her hand on it and said, 'Well, I guess we'll find out who knows what's going on today when Mrs Hunter tells us who got the part of Princess Penelope, won't we, Allie?'

So. She didn't know yet after all. The reason she'd

been all mad when she'd stomped up to us had been because the cool fifth-grade girls had been paying attention to us and not to her. That was all.

'I guess we will,' I said. I added in my head, but not out loud, *And it's going to be me*. The reason I didn't say it out loud was because I didn't want to make Sophie feel bad. I knew how much she wanted to play Princess Penelope, and that she was probably going to cry when she found out I'd gotten the part and not her. *Friends don't try to make friends feel bad on purpose*. That's a rule.

That was also why Cheyenne wasn't our friend. She was always trying to make us feel bad. And none of us had ever done anything to her except try to be nice.

I couldn't wait until Mrs Hunter told everyone I had gotten the part of Princess Penelope. Sure, it was going to be sad when Sophie cried.

But it was going to be *awesome* when Cheyenne did. And this time, her tears wouldn't be fake.

Rule #7

No One Likes a Sore Winner

'I hate her,' Sophie said after Cheyenne had stormed off.

'No you don't,' Erica, always the peacemaker, said. 'It's wrong to say you hate people. Even Cheyenne.'

Except that I didn't think so. And neither did Sophie, it turned out.

'I still hate her,' Sophie said. 'If she gets the part of Princess Penelope, I'm transferring to a different school.'

Oh no! Did this mean if *I* got the part, Sophie would transfer?

'What if Dominique gets it?' I asked carefully, as an experiment.

'She won't get it,' Sophie said with a sniff. 'Her audition stank.'

Uh-oh. This was terrible. If Mrs Hunter gave me

the part – and she was probably going to – one of my best friends was going to stop being my best friend, and maybe even transfer to another school! Oh, why had I even listened to Uncle Jay and auditioned for Princess Penelope in the first place? Uncle Jay gave the worst advice of all time. Well, some of the time.

It was right after that that the bell rang for us to go inside. As we got into our lines, Mrs Hunter noticed me looking at her and she smiled. I thought this must mean I got the part of Princess Penelope, but my hopes were crushed when all Mrs Hunter said was, 'I saw your mother last night on television, Allie. She was wonderful.'

Wonderful! Mrs Hunter thought my mother had been wonderful on TV! And she'd said so in front of the whole class! So loudly that Joey Fields went, 'Your mom was on TV, Allie? Why didn't you tell me?' And Stuart Maxwell tried to snatch my scarf off and throw it down the stairwell as we were going up the stairs, but Rosemary caught it just in time and gave it back to me.

'Your mom was good,' Rosemary said. 'But her eyes looked kinda funny.'

I stared at her. 'What?'

'Her eyes looked funny,' Rosemary said. 'Like a mouse or something.'

'They did not,' I said.

'All right,' Rosemary said. 'I'm just saying. There's nothing wrong with mice.'

What was Rosemary talking about? My mother looked nothing like a mouse. OK, maybe she looked prettier in real life than she had on TV. But everyone did. I looked different in mirrors than I did in my school photos, didn't I (usually better, since school photographers always seem to catch me smiling all goofy)?

Anyway, Mrs Hunter saying my mother looked wonderful on TV was a good sign that I'd gotten the part of Princess Penelope. I mean, wasn't it? Otherwise wouldn't she have just said my mom had done a good job or been nice or something. Wonderful means delightful, which is like joy, and Mrs Hunter had once said I was a *joy* to have in the classroom. So that's practically like saying I got the part.

Then Mrs Hunter was asking us to please take our seats, that she had an announcement to make. We all knew what that meant:

She was going to announce the cast list for *Princess Penelope in the Realm of Recycling*.

You could have heard Uncle Jay microwaving left-over pizza in his apartment over on campus six blocks away, that's how quiet it was in Room 209 as

Mrs Hunter unfolded the cast list. Everyone was dying to hear what part they had gotten.

'First,' Mrs Hunter said, 'allow me to tell you what a spectacular job I thought all of you did at the auditions yesterday. You were very prepared and you tried very hard, and I really appreciate that. I wish I could have given all of you the parts you wanted, but I couldn't, so instead I gave each of you the part at which I believe, knowing all of you as well as I do, you will most excel, and give the best performance. I really hope you will accept my decision. Now, I'll start with the evil queen's soldiers.'

There were hoots and fist pumps of excitement as Stuart Maxwell, Patrick Day, a few other boys, plus Rosemary all discovered they'd gotten the parts they'd wanted (well, Patrick and Stuart weren't too stoked to find out Rosemary was going to be a soldier along with them, since that meant they wouldn't be able to get in as much trouble as they would have liked. But she was sure excited).

Mrs Hunter then moved on to the reusable-water-bottle wizard, the part Joey Fields had really wanted. Not surprisingly, given that Joey F was the only one who'd auditioned for it, he got the part. Joey closed his eyes and gave a silent *Yessss!*

Next, Lenny Hsu learned he'd gotten the part of

the recycled-paper dragon (again, he'd been the only person who'd auditioned for it). He barely looked up from his book on dinosaurs on learning this.

Caroline looked relieved when she learned she was playing the unplug-when-not-in-use unicorn. This was the part she'd auditioned for. It had very few lines, exactly what Caroline wanted. She just had to prance around the stage and point Princess Penelope in the right direction through the magical woods with her horn, then explain that unplugging electronics when not in use saves a 1,000 pounds of carbon dioxide and 256 dollars per year per household. I guess Mrs Hunter had been as impressed by Caroline's prancing as we all were, since she gave Caroline the part.

But then Mrs Hunter read off some names of people who most definitely were *not* happy with the parts they'd gotten . . . like some of the girls who'd auditioned for the part of Princess Penelope. They were stunned to discover that instead of the princess they'd been awarded parts as public-transportation elves or water-conservation mermaids. Dominique and Marianne looked like they were about to cry on learning that they were compact-fluorescent-bulb fairies. I saw Cheyenne throwing them fake sympathetic smiles. I knew they were fake, because Cheyenne is incapable of feeling real sympathy for anyone but herself. I knew she was just waiting to hear her own name read off, along with the words, 'will be playing the part of Princess Penelope.'

Well, as far as I was concerned, Cheyenne could wait until the cows came home, but Mrs Hunter was *never* going to say those words. Because that part was mine.

Then Mrs Hunter said, 'The part of the fairy godmother of reusable-cloth shopping bags will be played by Erica Harrington.'

Erica gasped, and then twisted around in her seat to look at me. 'Yay!' she mouthed joyfully.

'Yay!' I mouthed back. I was really happy for Erica, because she'd wanted to play the fairy godmother so badly.

'The part of the fairy queen,' Mrs Hunter went on, 'will be played by Cheyenne O'Malley.'

Cheyenne wasn't the only person in Room 209 who gasped on hearing this – but she might have been the only person in the room who didn't gasp in a good way. You could tell she was totally horrified.

'Mrs Hunter,' Cheyenne said, her hand flying up into the air, 'I'm afraid there's been some mistake. That's not the part I auditioned for. I tried out for Princess Penelope!'

'I realize that, Cheyenne,' Mrs Hunter said. 'But I

think, based on your performance yesterday, that you'll be better in the role of the fairy queen, which is a very good part as well.'

Cheyenne's mouth fell open. Also, her eyes bulged out of her head a little.

'But that's not the *lead*,' Cheyenne said. 'I've always had the lead in every play I've been in. Back in Canada, anyway.'

'Well, I pictured you as the fairy queen from the play's inception,' Mrs Hunter said. 'It's a lovely part. You'll be able to wear lots of sparkles and a pair of wings, along with a beautiful gown and a tiara of compact-fluorescent light bulbs. Plus, you'll be the head of all the other fairies.'

The other fairies, Marianne and Dominique, looked over at Cheyenne expectantly, as if to say, *Hey! Remember us? We wanted to play Princess Penelope and we're stuck with being compact-fluorescent-bulb fairies too. Hello!* I mean, at least Cheyenne got to be a compact-fluorescent-bulb fairy *queen*.

But Cheyenne barely glanced at them.

'I don't want to be a fairy queen,' Cheyenne said. 'I want to be Princess Penelope. And I'm telling my mother!'

With that, she folded her arms across her chest,

turned her head to look out the window, and dismissed us all.

Mrs Hunter said, 'Well, I'm sorry to hear that. Do let your mother know that I look forward to hearing from her, as always,' and returned to her list.

There were only two names she hadn't read off yet – mine and Sophie's. And I knew why.

Obviously I'd gotten the role of Princess Penelope. I couldn't think what other part hadn't been assigned yet, but clearly Sophie was getting that one . . .

. . . and just as clearly, she was going to cry when she found out I was Princess Penelope and she wasn't.

So I couldn't act too excited when I found out. Even though, of course, on the inside I would be bursting with happiness.

No one likes a sore loser like Cheyenne. That's a rule.

But *No one likes a sore winner* either. That's another rule.

So if you win, it's rude to be too celebratory about it and rub it in other people's faces. It's important to accept victory modestly.

Then *You can celebrate all you want in private, where the losers can't see you* (that's another rule).

'Allie Finkle . . .' Mrs Hunter read from her list. I leaned forward a little in my chair, trying to contain myself. I wasn't going to jump to my feet or any-thing, let alone climb on top of my desk and do a self-congratulatory victory dance.

But I might do one tiny fist pump. Just a little one. I mean, I could celebrate a *little*. After all, I'd earned it. I'd worked hard on that audition!

'. . . I'm giving you the part of the evil queen,' Mrs Hunter said.

Yay –

Wait. What?

What had she just said?

'Cool, Allie,' Rosemary, down the row of desks from me, whispered. 'We'll get to be in tons of scenes together!'

'And the role of Princess Penelope,' Mrs Hunter went on, 'goes to Sophie Abramowitz.'

Sophie, in her seat a few rows ahead of mine, let out a little shriek. Then she put both hands over her mouth and said, 'Oh my goodness! Oh . . . my goodness! Me? *ME?*'

'Yes, Sophie,' Mrs Hunter said, smiling at her. 'You. Now, class. We don't have very much time. I want everyone to start trying to learn their lines right away. I want them memorized by the end of next week at the latest. Now, let's get out our maths books and turn to page two-ten. We're going to be working on fractions this morning.'

Except that I didn't get out my maths book. And I didn't turn it to page 210.

Because I couldn't move. I just couldn't believe it. I mean, I just *couldn't believe it*. I'd tried out for the role of Princess Penelope – I'd worked really, really hard on my audition – and yet somehow I'd ended up as the princess's *evil stepmother*?

How could something like that even happen?

I mean, no offence, but I had been the best Princess Penelope at the auditions. I'm not even being a braggart either, when I say that. I had practised with an actual theatre major (well, at one time). Uncle Jay had totally coached me. I hadn't overacted like Cheyenne. And I had even made Mrs Hunter laugh during my audition!

And OK, maybe she wasn't supposed to have laughed. But come on!

And I know I don't look like a princess as Sophie does. I'm not totally beautiful in the traditional sense, the way she is.

But I *know* I'm a better actress. I'm not saying that to be mean. And I would never say it to Sophie's face.

But that doesn't change the fact that it's true. And I know it.

So why would Mrs Hunter – *my* Mrs Hunter, the best teacher I'd ever had – give me the *worst part in the whole entire play*? The part of the evil, mean sorceress who spends the play trying to kill not only the pretty heroine, but everyone else in the Realm of Recycling. A character who litters. A character who thinks global warming doesn't exist even though ninety-eight per cent of scientists do and who doesn't realize you can save a tree by recycling a stack of newspapers only three feet high. The character everyone hates. Why? WHY?

It didn't make any sense. Had I done something to make Mrs Hunter hate me? I couldn't remember doing anything to make Mrs Hunter hate me. But maybe I had, by accident or something. Maybe I had disappointed her in some way, and so in revenge, or to teach me a lesson, she was making me take this awful, awful part.

Or maybe . . . maybe Mrs Hunter was mad at my mom. Maybe Mrs Hunter had really loved *Requiem for a Somnambulist* and was mad that my mom called it preachy and pretentious.

But no . . . that made no sense either. She had said my mom's performance on *Good News!* the night before had been wonderful. Why would she say that if she didn't agree with my mom's review?

No. It must be me. It must be *me* Mrs Hunter hated.

I wanted to cry. A few moments earlier, I had been telling myself not to celebrate too hard in order not to hurt my best friend's feelings.

And now I was sitting there, trying hard not to burst into tears in front of the whole class.

Only not really, because no one was even paying attention to me. Everyone was too busy buzzing about Sophie and her remarkable achievement.

And Sophie was being fittingly modest, acting just the way a proper princess should, saying, 'Oh, thanks,' and, 'Well, I'm just going to do my best,' and, 'It's all Mrs Hunter's doing, really, for giving me the chance.'

I'm sorry, but even though I know it's wrong to hate people, a part of me hated Sophie just then!

Well, OK, maybe not. But a part of me really disliked her. Just a little. Because that should have been me saying those things! How come no one was crowding around *my* desk, congratulating me?

Oh, wait. I know why. Because everyone hates the evil queen!

To prove it, Stuart Maxwell just threw a wadded up piece of paper at me and went, 'Ha. Evil queen. That suits you, Allie!'

I wanted to cry even harder when he said that. But instead, remembering I was an actress, I *acted* like I didn't want to cry. I said, 'Well, you're an evil soldier. And you work for me, the evil queen. So you have to do what I say.'

He looked at me with his eyebrows raised and went, 'You can't tell me what to do.'

'Yes I can,' I said. 'I'm the queen. So I'm the boss of you.'

Defenceless in the face of such logic, Stuart did the only thing he could, which was take out a piece of paper and frantically start drawing headless zombies on it.

I kind of knew how he felt. I mean, I would have started drawing headless zombies too, if I thought it would have made me feel better.

But I knew the only thing that was going to make me feel better was . . . well, getting to play Princess Penelope.

But since I knew that wasn't going to happen now, I guessed I was going to have to settle for going up to Sophie myself when the bell for morning recess rang, and saying, 'Hey, Sophie. Congratulations. I'm really glad you got the part you wanted.'

And act like I meant it.

Which was exactly what I did. While Cheyenne stomped off to go call her mother on her cellphone and tell her to call Mrs Hunter, I went up to Sophie and congratulated her for getting the role of Princess Penelope. The role I thought I should have gotten.

Because that's what gracious losers – and best friends – do.

'Oh my goodness, Allie,' Sophie said, throwing her arms around my neck and giving me a huge hug. 'Thank you so much! And I'm so sorry you didn't get it. You were really good too.'

'Yeah,' Caroline said. 'But it's OK, because Allie didn't really want it the way you did, Sophie. She just tried for it to make sure Cheyenne didn't get it.'

I practically had to blink back tears when I heard that. I hadn't wanted it as much as Sophie? Um, yes, I so totally had.

But, considering I hadn't gotten it, I guess it was just as well everyone thought this.

'Yeah,' I said casually, hugging Sophie back. 'I'm fine with the part I got. I mean, it's not like I'm going to go call my mother and complain, like Cheyenne.'

'Can you believe she's doing that?' Sophie let go of me and pushed some of her curly hair out of her big brown eyes. 'Talk about being a princess! She must think she is one, or something!'

'Totally,' I said.

'You'll make such a good evil queen, Allie,' Erica said. 'You'll be the best evil queen ever.'

I just stared at her. 'I will?'

'Of course,' Sophie said.

'You're always the best when we play queens at recess,' Caroline said, seeming to agree with Sophie and Erica. 'Why wouldn't you make a great *evil* queen? And you know Stuart and those guys will do what you say.'

My shoulders sagged. 'Oh,' I said. 'That's right.' No wonder Mrs Hunter had given me the part of the evil queen! It wasn't because she hated me. It was so the boys playing the evil soldiers would obey me. I sat next to them all day, didn't I? Well, me and Rosemary. She probably thought Rosemary and I would keep them in line at rehearsals the same way we did all day in the classroom.

Well, it wasn't fair! Just once, I wanted to get to play the part of the pretty princess, instead of the tough girl who keeps the bad boys in line.

But I guess that was never going to happen. At least, not with this play. And not with this teacher. All my hopes had been raised that, for once, things might turn out differently, only to be dashed.

And I knew exactly who to blame for that. For the raised hopes, anyway.

Rule #8

There Are No Small Parts.
Only Small Actors

I found him at our house after school, with his head in our refrigerator – a place, I would like to add, where one could usually find Uncle Jay when he wasn't in class, delivering pizzas, out with his girlfriend, or watching the show *COPS* on his TV in his apartment.

'How long has it been since your parents went to the grocery store?' Uncle Jay asked me when I came into the kitchen. He took a big bite out of an apple. 'You're out of apples. Well, I mean, now. This is the last one. And I really had to scour the place to find it.'

I slammed my bookbag down on the counter and glared at him.

'What?' he said. He held out the apple, which had a big bite taken out of it. 'Did you want it?'

'I didn't get the part of Princess Penelope,' I said, 'and it's all your fault!'

'My fault?' Uncle Jay looked shocked. 'How is it *my* fault? Did you figure out what Princess Penelope had for breakfast?'

'Yes.' I was practically crying, I was so mad. 'Count Chocula. And I still didn't get the part.'

'Did you pro*ject*?' Uncle Jay asked.

'Yes, I pro*jected*,' I said. 'And if you ask me, that was the exact problem. I pro*jected* so much, I think I probably came off as too loud and queenly, and not soft and princessy enough. So Mrs Hunter gave Sophie the part of the princess, and me the part of the evil queen!' I didn't mention the part about how she'd probably given it to me so I could keep Stuart and Patrick in line. I figured Uncle Jay didn't have to know *everything*. Just enough to make him feel bad for what he'd done. 'I have to be the princess's evil stepmother, who doesn't believe in recycling or saving the planet!'

Uncle Jay took another bite of his apple and looked thoughtful. 'A character part,' he said. 'Hmmm. I could see you in one of those, actually.'

'What's a character part?' I demanded. I wasn't going to let him distract me from being mad at him though. I had to take out my anger and disappointment over not getting the role of Princess Penelope on someone, and Uncle Jay seemed like the best person for that.

'A character part,' Uncle Jay said, pulling up a

kitchen counter stool and sitting on it, 'is a support-ing role, often comic in nature. The main character's sidekick or sometimes her mortal enemy.'

'I don't get it,' I said. My face felt hot from trying not to cry.

'An example would be Sebastian to Ariel in *The Little Mermaid*,' Uncle Jay said, 'or Ursula, the sea witch.'

My eyes filled up with tears. Trying not to cry wasn't working any more. I had been holding back sobs all day. And now, finally, since I was home, it was safe to let them go. None of my friends was around, so I didn't have to put on a brave face any more. Cheyenne was back at school, having a meeting with Mrs Hunter, Mrs Jenkins the principal, and Mrs O'Malley over her not getting the part of Princess Penelope. Sophie was frantic that Mrs Jenkins was going to force Mrs Hunter to give Cheyenne the role of Princess Penelope. But Erica, Caroline and I had spent the walk home assuring her this wouldn't happen.

And the whole time, all I'd wanted to do was cry myself, over my own disappointment.

Well, now I finally could.

So I did.

'That's just it,' I wailed. 'I don't *want* to play a sea witch. *Or* a crab! I wanted to be a p-princess!'

'Hey.' Uncle Jay looked concerned – and super surprised – at my outburst. 'It's OK. It's much cooler to be a queen than a princess anyway.'

'An ee-ee-evil queen!' I reminded him, choking a little on my own tears.

'What are you so upset about?' Uncle Jay wanted to know. 'Everyone likes Ursula much better than they like Ariel anyway.'

'No, they d-don't. She's the evil witch who takes away the little mermaid's voice. Everyone hates Ursula. When she dies at the end, everyone is happy.'

'That means she did a fantastic job at her perform-ance,' Uncle Jay said. 'Don't you get it, Allie? Ursula isn't real. She's a character played by an actress. An actress who did such a good job developing her char-acter and then performing her that she makes the audience hate her. That's an incredible skill. It's easy to play someone everyone is naturally going to love right away, just by the nature of who she is, a beautiful princess. Anybody can do that. But the fact that your teacher saw something in you that told her, Hey, this little girl could do something really challenging – make people hate her – means that she must think you're the best actress in your whole class.'

I stared at him through my tears. The truth was, I had never thought of the evil queen that way – as a challenging role. I had just thought of it as the worst role in the whole entire play. Which it was, naturally. Unless . . .

'Really?' I wiped my eyes with the back of one of my wrists. 'Do you really think Mrs Hunter thinks I'm a good actress?'

'She must,' Uncle Jay said. 'Directors don't assign character roles to bad actors. They're extremely difficult to pull off. What exactly happened during your audition? Think. Did Mrs Hunter do or say anything unusual?'

'Well.' I tried to think. 'She laughed once . . .'

Uncle Jay snapped his fingers and pointed at me. 'That's it. She laughed. Did she laugh when anyone else auditioned?'

'No,' I said. 'It was a serious scene. It wasn't supposed to be funny.'

'So you must have good comic timing,' Uncle Jay said. 'Let me see the script again.'

I unzipped my backpack and handed it to him. 'I still don't see,' I said to him, 'how getting the role of someone evil is a good thing.'

'Shh,' Uncle Jay said as he flipped through the

script. 'Yes.' He nodded as he read over my lines. 'Oh yes. I can see what she's doing.'

I leaned forward on my counter stool. 'What?'

'You realize,' he said, 'that you have a lot more lines as the queen than you would have had as the princess.'

'I do?' This piece of information caused my eyes, still teary, to bug out a bit.

'A lot more,' Uncle Jay said. 'I'd even go so far as to say that the evil queen, and not Princess Penelope, is the real star of the show.'

'But she's evil, and she dies at the end,' I informed him.

'That's right,' Uncle Jay said, brightening up even more. 'You have a death scene, don't you? That's even better! You ought to really be able to milk that. Allie, this is brilliant. You're going to steal the show.'

'I don't know what you're talking about,' I said, my shoulders sagging. 'I have to play a stinking evil queen, who doesn't recycle. Are you even listening to me?'

'Of course I am,' Uncle Jay said, handing the script back to me. 'Now, here's what you need to do first. Find your character's motivation. Figure out what made Princess Penelope's stepmother so evil in the first place. Get to the heart of her evilness, find out what makes her tick – and you'll be able to give the performance of your life.'

I stared at him some more. 'I don't understand anything you're talking about,' I said. 'Nothing made her evil. She's just evil.'

'Of course something made her evil,' Uncle Jay said. 'No one is born evil. People learn to be evil because of things that happen to them in their lives. What happened to Princess Penelope's stepmother that made her the way she is? And by the way, I think you need to give her a name. You can't just keep calling her the evil queen. You need to get to know her if you're going to play her properly. Find out –'

'– what she eats for breakfast,' I said tiredly.

I couldn't believe Uncle Jay was making such a big deal over an evil queen. Who even cared what she had for breakfast, or what her real name was? She was evil! I was the one playing her, and I didn't even care. I was still mad about the whole thing . . . that I wasn't going to get to wear my gold flower-girl dress now. What kind of costume would an evil queen wear, anyway? Something black, I supposed. What was he getting so excited about for, anyway? People were going to boo, not clap, for me. Because I was evil. Couldn't he see the unfairness of it all? I had worked so hard, and not gotten the part I wanted. I mean, that wasn't how things were supposed to go. I didn't agree with Cheyenne calling her mother, and her mother demanding a meeting with Mrs Hunter and the principal.

But I understood how she felt.

It was kind of funny that right then my mom walked in from outside, where she'd apparently been doing some gardening. At least, she was pulling off her gardening gloves and windcheater.

'Oh, hello, Allie, I thought I saw you come home,' she said. Then she noticed my face and looked sort of alarmed. 'Honey, what's the matter?'

'She didn't get the lead in her class play,' Uncle Jay answered for me. 'And she's a little upset. But I told her not to worry. All she needs to do is find her character's motivation and she'll be fine.'

'Oh, Allie,' Mom said, coming up and putting her arms around me. 'I'm so sorry. You must be so disappointed. Is there anything I can do?'

Even though it felt good to be hugged, I tensed up.

'Don't call the school!' I cried. 'I don't want you to call Mrs Jenkins to complain!'

'Why on earth would I call your principal to complain?' Mom asked, letting go of me.

'Because that's what Cheyenne's mom did,' I said. 'They're having a meeting in Mrs Jenkins's office with

Mrs Hunter right now, all because Cheyenne didn't get the part of Princess Penelope.'

'Was that the part you wanted?' Mom asked, pushing a loose strand of my hair out of my eyes.

'Yes,' I said. I was trying to keep a brave face on. It was pretty hard though. 'But Sophie got it. Which is good, because she deserved it. She was really good at the audition. And she looks like a princess.'

'So do you,' Mom said, laying a hand on my cheek.

'Well,' I said. I suddenly felt like crying again, but I tried really hard to hold it back. This, by the way, is called acting. 'I guess Mrs Hunter doesn't think so. She gave me the part of the princess's evil stepmother, who spends the whole play trying to kill her and then gets killed at the end with her own evil pollution ray.'

My mom got a funny look on her face, kind of like she was trying not to laugh. But I didn't exactly see anything humorous about the situation.

'Oh, honey,' Mom said 'I'm so sorry. You've had a terrible day, haven't you?'

'Well,' I said, 'it hasn't been great.'

'Tell you what,' Mom said. 'I was thinking about going to the mall. Why don't you come along? We'll make it a girls' afternoon out.'

This caused me to feel a little bit better. 'Really?' I brightened up. 'No boys?'

'No boys,' Mom said. 'Just you and me.'

I jumped off the counter stool and ran to get my coat, joining Mom at the back door where she was grabbing her purse and car keys. Uncle Jay, not done giving advice, called after me, 'Don't forget . . . Stanislavski said, "There are no small parts, only small actors"!'

'What does he mean by that?' I asked as I followed Mom out to her car.

'Well,' Mom said, 'that you should be happy with the part Mrs Hunter gave you. Otherwise, you might seem ungrateful.'

Oh. So *There are no small parts, only small actors* was a rule.

I got into the car and pulled my seat belt tight. 'I'm happy I'm in the play,' I said. 'I just wish I had Sophie's part. Or even Cheyenne's part. She's playing the fairy queen.'

'I know, honey,' Mom said as she started backing the car out of the driveway. 'Sometimes we don't get the things we want. That's just the way things work out. So we have to try to find the good in the things we do have. There must be something good about playing the princess's stepmother.'

As hard as I tried, I couldn't think of anything good about playing the evil queen. And said so.

'Try harder,' Mom said. 'What kind of character is she?'

'Well,' I said. 'She's a queen.'

'There you go!' Mom said brightly, from behind the wheel. 'A queen! Well, that's terrific! You love queens. We'll make you a fabulous queen costume. With a really big crown.'

'I should probably have a cape,' I said as I watched the houses near where we live go by. 'Queens always have capes.'

'We'll make you a cape,' Mom said. 'How about the cape Daddy wore when he was Dracula for Halloween a few years ago? We could cut it down to fit you.'

I thought about Dad's Dracula cape. It had a high pointy collar at the neck that stood up on its own. Come to think of it, it looked quite queenly.

'Yes,' I said. 'That would look really good. And I think I should wear that dress you wore to the Hausers' pool party last year.'

Mom looked at me in the rear-view mirror again. Both her eyebrows were raised. 'My black terry cloth pool cover-up?'

'Yes,' I said. It was made of terry cloth. But it looked like velvet. And on me, it was a long dress. As I had discovered one night when I'd tried it on when Mom wasn't home and Caroline, Erica, Sophie, Rosemary and I had played Fashion Show with her clothes.

'Well,' Mom said, 'I suppose you can wear that. If you really want to . . .'

By the time we got to the mall, we had my evil-queen costume all planned out. We didn't even have to buy anything, because everything I needed we already owned, or could make with things we had in the house. We went into the big department store, because there were a few things Mom wanted to pick up for herself, though. She headed right to the make-up counter.

'Hi,' a very pretty lady behind the make-up counter said to her. 'What can I do for you today? You know we're having a special on—'

'That's very nice,' Mom interrupted, even though she says *It's rude to interrupt people*. That's a rule. 'But I need something to make my eyes look . . . more defined.'

'Oh, that's easy,' the lady behind the counter said. 'Here, let me show you these new products we just got in. You're going to love them. They're hypo-allergenic and completely smudge-proof, but very easy to remove at the end of the day.'

My mom sat down on the stool the make-up lady pulled out. She said, 'Allie, don't go far,' when I wandered over to a display of headbands and started looking at them.

'I won't,' I said. 'But I might go over to the pet shop and see if they have any of those new breakaway collars. Because those are better for cats than the one I got for Mewsie when he was a baby.'

'No,' Mom said. The make-up lady was already putting stuff on her eyes, so Mom had to hold still. 'We'll go look at them when I'm done. I'll just be a minute.'

'OK,' I said, and went over to a nearby counter to check out the sparkly jewellery, pretending I really was a queen (not an evil one though) and could afford to buy whatever I wanted. I was deciding between a fancy watch that showed the sun, moon and stars on the face and a diamond pendant shaped like a French poodle, when I heard a familiar voice go, 'But, Mom! I *want* them!'

I froze where I was standing and looked across the aisle. Sure enough, there she was: Cheyenne O'Malley, the fairy queen herself, shopping with a lady I was sure had to be *her* mother.

Rule #9

Best Friends Rescue Each
Other When Someone's Evil
Sister Has Them Trapped

Cheyenne and her mom were looking down at a glass case of jewellery just like the one I was standing next to.

Only Cheyenne hadn't noticed me yet, since all her attention was on the earrings she was looking at. I shrank behind a spinning rack of jewellery on top of the case beside me, so she hopefully wouldn't see me. I just didn't really feel like talking to Cheyenne right then. I mean, I didn't feel like talking to her when I was *in* school. Why would I feel like talking to Cheyenne *outside* school?

'Those earrings are a hundred dollars, Cheyenne,' Mrs O'Malley said. 'That's too expensive.'

'I don't care,' Cheyenne said in a rude voice – the kind of voice that, if I'd ever used with my mom, would have gotten me sent to my room. With no dessert. 'They're really cute. And they'll be perfect with my purple top.'

'But you have a pair just like them,' Mrs O'Malley said.

'Yeah,' Cheyenne said. 'But I lost them. Remember?'

'Oh, Cheyenne.' Mrs O'Malley let out a sigh. 'Why can't you learn to be more responsible?'

Cheyenne got a look on her face that I recognized. It was her 'Now I'm going to start crying' look. I wondered if she was thinking about the Jonas Brothers concert her mom had failed to get tickets for.

'*Mo-o-om*,' she practically yelled. A couple of people shopping nearby looked over. I hoped they didn't wonder why I was crouching behind a jewellery stand. I pretended to be really, really interested in a pair of earrings shaped like violins, even though I don't have pierced ears. Or play the violin.

'Cheyenne, that's enough,' Mrs O'Malley said pleadingly.

'Shut up!' Cheyenne yelled at her mom. 'You couldn't even get the part of Princess Penelope for me! The least you can do is get me *these*!'

I couldn't believe Cheyenne had said *shut up* to her mom. If *I* had ever said that to *my* mom – or tried yelling at her like that . . . well, I wouldn't get what I wanted. That was for sure.

'Oh, for heaven's sake, Cheyenne,' Mrs O'Malley said. She signalled to a saleslady, who came right over. 'Could we look at these, please?' Mrs O'Malley asked, pointing at whatever it was Cheyenne wanted (that cost a hundred dollars) from inside the display case.

'We'll take them,' Cheyenne said, before the saleslady had even had a chance to get them out.

'Cheyenne,' her mother said. But she was laughing, like, *Isn't she adorable?*, not using her *You're-going-to-get-it-if-you-don't-use-a-different-tone-with-me-young-lady* voice the way *my* mother would have been if I'd been as rude to her as Cheyenne was being.

'Here you are,' the saleslady said, and she laid a pair of purple sparky earrings down on the counter in front of Cheyenne. 'They're genuine amethyst.'

No way! Cheyenne was getting a new pair of hundred-dollar genuine amethyst earrings, and it wasn't even her birthday or Christmas? Just because she'd looked like she was going to cry when her mother had said no?

If I had ever tried something like that, my mother would have made me go sit in the car.

Well, no, she wouldn't really. But only because Child Protective Services would arrest her.

But she'd at least have taken away my TV privileges for a week.

Wow! Things were sure different at Cheyenne's house than they were at my house. I guess the rule at Cheyenne's house was, *If you whine enough about it, you'll get what you want.*

Whereas the rule at my house was, *If you whine about it, you'll get sent to your room and also have your TV privileges suspended and maybe also no dessert and possibly also your Nintendo DS taken away for a week.*

'Well?' Mrs O'Malley asked her daughter. 'What do you think?'

'They're all right,' Cheyenne said with a sigh. 'But playing Princess Penelope would be better.'

'Well,' Mrs O'Malley said, handing the saleslady her credit card, 'that isn't going to happen.'

'Because Mrs Hunter is a big—'

'Now, Cheyenne,' Mrs O'Malley said, finally using a warning voice. 'Remember what Mrs Jenkins said. You can't always have the lead in the play every time.'

'Even if I'm the best?' Cheyenne demanded.

'Even if you're the best,' Mrs O'Malley said. 'You need to let some of the other little girls have a turn.'

I felt my face turning red. This was ridiculous! Cheyenne wasn't the best!

And it was horrible that Mrs O'Malley was standing there saying that she was. Even if she *was* her mother.

'Come on,' Mrs O'Malley said, taking the bag the saleslady handed to her, then giving Cheyenne a fond hug, 'let's go get some ice cream. Would you like that?'

'I guess,' Cheyenne said, not looking very excited. 'But none of that crummy frozen yogurt. I want real ice cream.'

'Of course,' Mrs O'Malley said with a sigh as they walked away.

Ice cream? Cheyenne gets hundred-dollar amethyst earrings *and* ice cream? My mom won't even let me get pierced ears until I'm thirteen, let alone ice cream before dinner.

'Hi, honey.'

My mom, coming up behind me, scared the life out of me. I jumped so high in the air I almost knocked over the earring rack.

'Are you all right?' Mom asked. 'What were you doing down there, anyway?'

'Oh, n-nothing,' I said. 'Just looking at these, um, earrings.'

'But you don't even have pierced ears.' Mom looked confused.

'I know,' I said. Cheyenne and her mom had fortunately disappeared around the corner. 'I was just . . . can we go look at cat collars now?'

'Of course.'

We bought a special collar with a Velcro fastener for Mewsie, so if he was ever climbing a tree (not that I ever let him outside, but in case I ever do) and a branch slipped between his collar and his neck, the collar would break away and he wouldn't choke to death, a frequent cause of death in cats, at least according to Sophie, who is always telling us horrible stories about ways you could die. In honour of Kevin, I chose a pirate collar with skulls and crossbones on it. I figured Mewsie, being a boy cat, might like it better than the pink sparkle collar he currently wore.

Over the weekend, Rosemary, Caroline, Sophie, Erica and I got together at Erica's house to practise our parts for the play. Erica had some fairy wings left over from a Halloween costume Missy had once worn, so she put them on, and Mom had fished Dad's Dracula cape out for me (even though she hadn't had a chance to cut it down yet), so I wore that. Rosemary had a sword one of her brothers let her borrow, Sophie had a tiara she found somewhere, and Caroline taped an empty toilet-paper roll to her forehead to make it look like she was a unicorn.

We acted out our parts very dramatically, if you ask me. So dramatically that Missy came into Erica's room three times to ask us to quit being so dramatic, even though we told her (very politely) that we were doing something school-related and that we *had* to be loud.

The third time she came into Erica's room, Missy yelled, 'You guys!' (She kind of spat when she said the word *guys*, because of her braces.) 'I'm trying to talk to my friend Stacy! She's going through a real hard time right now because her boyfriend just texted her that he's breaking up with her. So can you please *shut up*?'

After that we decided instead of play practice it would be more fun to spy on Missy's phone conversation, even though Erica didn't think we should, because Missy would be madder than ever if she found out.

But we all swore we wouldn't get caught since we'd be quieter than mice.

So when we finally got Erica to agree, we all crawled into the hallway and huddled outside Missy's door and heard her going, 'Uh-huh? And then what did he say? And then what did you say? Well, then what did he say? Well, then what did you say? Well, then what did *he* say?' which was fun for a while, but then got kind of boring . . .

. . . until Rosemary got the idea we should a shove a paper clip through the big old-fashioned keyhole of Missy's door and let it drop down to the other side, inside Missy's room. Just to see if she'd notice.

So we did . . . and Missy totally didn't notice! Maybe because she was so involved in talking to her friend Stacy and all, and helping her through her big break-up.

So then after some coaxing from us, Erica went and got some more paper clips. And then we all took turns shoving them through Missy's keyhole. *Plink! Plink!* they went as they hit the wood floor beneath Missy's door. When we laid down, we could see them beneath the door, piling up right there on top of each other!

But Missy wasn't paying any attention. She just kept going, 'Well, obviously, you deserve better, Stace. You know what? You know what? He's beneath you, that's what. Let him have her if that's the type of girl he wants. If he wants to take her to the formal and not you, so what? She's not worth your crying over. Neither one of them is.'

Plink! Plink!

It was really, really hard not to give ourselves away by laughing. Sophie had to press both her hands over her mouth so no laugh noises escaped. I have to admit it had been kind of hard for me to start liking Sophie again, after her getting the part of Princess Penelope and not me. I mean, I didn't want to be jealous, because she was my friend. But a part of me totally was, when I thought about how I wasn't going to be able to wear my gold flower-girl dress on stage.

But as we slipped paper clip after paper clip through the keyhole, and Missy *still* didn't notice, Sophie looked so funny trying not to laugh, I couldn't help but start to feel a little friendly towards her again.

We were all holding our breath as Rosemary slipped about the fiftieth paper clip through Missy's keyhole when a voice behind us went, '*Girls. What are you doing?*'

We all jumped nearly out of our skins. Until we twirled around to see it was only Erica's older brother John standing there.

We sagged with relief that it wasn't Mr Harrington.

'Shh,' Erica said worriedly. 'We're slipping paper clips through Missy's keyhole. Don't tell.'

'Paper clips?' John made a face. 'What's the fun in that?'

'Well, what else are we going to put through there?' Rosemary wanted to know.

'Hang on a minute,' John said, and he disappeared

up the staircase to his room, which is in the Harringtons' refinished attic. A minute later he came back with a spray can with a special nozzle. 'Silly String,' he said.

Erica looked shocked. 'But she's totally going to notice that!'

'Isn't that the point?' John wanted to know. 'Step aside, ladies, and let the master do his work.'

We all moved over as John knelt down in front of his sister's bedroom door, put the can of Silly String up against the keyhole, then pressed the nozzle. We heard the *shhhhhhh* sound of a spray of Silly String being set loose.

Then we heard a scream from inside Missy's room.

'Retreat!' John yelled, jumping to his feet. 'Retreat, retreat!'

Screaming, we all began running in different directions as Missy tore open her bedroom door, shrieking, 'You . . . you . . . *ingrates*! Look what you've done to my floor! It's a mess!'

It's really hard to run when you're laughing so hard you can't see properly, because of the tears in your eyes. But I grabbed hold of a fistful of Rosemary's shirt and hoped wherever she was going, she'd just drag me there.

'Get back here!' Missy yelled, her voice sounding scarily closer. I couldn't see how close she'd gotten though, because my laugh tears were still keeping me from being able to see anything really. 'Get back here and clean this up!'

'She's coming!' Rosemary screamed hysterically. 'Run!'

I still had hold of Rosemary's shirt. We had almost made it to the safety of Erica's bedroom when suddenly someone stomped down on the back of Dad's cape, which I was still wearing. This yanked me backwards so hard that my feet flew out from under me. It also caused the ribbons that held Dad's cape tied around my neck to cut into my throat.

Suddenly my eyes weren't filled with laugh tears any more, but real tears. Because excuse me, that totally hurt!

Also, I was lying on my back, blinking up at a big blurry image I realized had to be Missy. Missy was the person who'd stepped on the back of my cape!

I was caught! By the enemy! By Missy!

'You little brat!' Missy snarled in my face. 'I can't believe it! Why are there paper clips all over my floor? You better get in there and clean it all up.'

'Allie!' I heard Sophie scream from somewhere that sounded far away. 'We've got to rescue Allie!'

'Troops,' I heard John yell, 'one of our men is down

and has been captured. We can't leave a fellow soldier in enemy hands!'

The next thing I knew, Silly String and paper clips
were flying everywhere. Most of the Silly String was
hitting Missy's shirt.

'John!' Missy screamed. 'I'm going to kill you! This
shirt is brand new from the Gap!'

'Here, Allie,' Sophie said, appearing from nowhere
and holding out a hand. 'We're here to rescue you!'

I grabbed the hand Sophie was offering and let her
pull me up, while Erica, Caroline and Rosemary
formed a huddle around us so Missy couldn't get us.
All of them were screaming. Caroline's toilet-paper-
roll unicorn horn was dangling off her forehead by a
single piece of tape, but she didn't appear to notice.

'Stay back,' John was yelling as he kept spraying
Missy with Silly String. 'Stay back, vile beast!'

'You are so dead,' Missy shrieked, trying to grab
John and put him in a headlock. 'I can't believe how
immature you're being.'

'You guys,' Erica yelled in alarm. 'Stop fighting!'

'Never!' John was blindly shooting Silly String
into the air now. 'Never give up! Never surrender!'

'Hey!' Mrs Harrington yelled up the stairs. 'What's
going on up there?'

We all froze. Only some of the Silly String John had

sprayed kept moving, falling softly from Missy's shirt to the top of John's head.

'Nothing,' we all called down to Mrs Harrington at the same time.

'Well, I think your friends have been over long enough, Erica,' Mrs Harrington replied from downstairs. 'It's time for them to go home now. I'm just about to take dinner off the stove. John, come down and set the table. It's your turn.'

'OK, Mrs Harrington,' Rosemary said sweetly. 'I'll call my parents to come pick me up right away.'

We waited until we heard Mrs Harrington's footsteps walking away. Then Missy said, 'Ha!' and knocked the canister of Silly String from John's hand before letting go of his head. 'You have to go set the table! Loser.'

'Takes one to know one,' John said, and with quiet dignity he brushed all the Silly String from his head. Then, seeing that I'd been successfully freed, he gave us all the two-fingered V sign for victory and said, 'We will fight again another day, troops,' and ran down the stairs.

Missy looked over at us, rolled her eyes and stomped back into her room. But not before saying, '*Ingrates*,' and slamming her door.

'That,' Caroline said, her toilet-paper-roll unicorn

horn bobbing as she spoke, 'was awesome. I wish I had an older brother.'

'No you don't,' Erica said mournfully. 'Usually *I'm* the one he sprays Silly String on.'

I turned to Sophie. I was sorry for feeling so jealous of her, over the Princess Penelope thing. She was a true friend after all, for rescuing me from Missy.

And it wasn't her fault she'd gotten the role instead of me. The best man (or woman) for the part had won. That was all.

'Thanks for rescuing me,' I said to her.

'Oh,' Sophie said, laughing. 'It was nothing.'

But it hadn't been nothing. Sophie had saved me from Missy's evil clutches. And all I'd done was entertain mean thoughts every now and then about her possibly falling down the stairs and breaking her leg and me getting to play Princess Penelope at the last minute.

Well, not any more. Because best friends don't think those kinds of thoughts about each other. *Best friends rescue each other when someone's evil sister has them trapped.*

That's a rule.

Rule #10

You Can't Make Someone with
a Bad Attitude About Something
Change Their Mind and Have a
Good One. You Just Can't

On Monday, when the time came for art class, Mrs Hunter asked everyone to take out their scripts for what she called our first 'read-through'. We were supposed to read through the script of *Princess Penelope in the Realm of Recycling* out loud, with everyone saying their lines the way they would during the play, but just while sitting at our desks, without doing what Mrs Hunter called the 'blocking', which was the moves we would make on the stage while we said our lines.

Not to brag, but I thought Rosemary, Erica, Caroline, Sophie and I did the best jobs of anyone reading out loud.

This was obviously because of all the practising we'd done over the weekend. It had really paid off.

Some people, though – it became clear as the week

progressed and we moved from doing read-throughs to actually doing real rehearsals downstairs on the stage in the auditorium slash gym slash cafeteria – weren't taking their parts very seriously. You would think I'd be talking about the boys, such as Patrick Day and Stuart Maxwell, but I actually meant Cheyenne. The only thing I could figure out was that she still hadn't gotten over not being given the part of Princess Penelope, and so she just read off the lines of the compact-fluorescent-bulb fairy queen in a sing-songy voice that almost seemed to say, 'Yeah, I'm here and I'm reading these lines, but I'm not actually going to *act them out*, or put any effort at all into playing this part.'

Marianne and Dominique did basically the same thing (only they were such bad actresses anyway you couldn't really tell).

I, on the other hand, really went for it, each and every rehearsal – though I was still bothered by what Uncle Jay had said about how I had to figure out what Princess Penelope's stepmother's motivation was. I honestly didn't have the slightest idea. Why *was* she so evil – especially if what Uncle Jay had said was true, that no one is actually born bad? And why *did* the queen hate recycling so much?

I still wasn't sure what had happened to Princess Penelope's stepmother to make her the way she was.

But thanks to what had happened at Erica's house, I was pretty sure I had figured out what her name was: it was Queen Melissa the Maleficent!

In fact, every time I read her lines out loud (Queen Melissa the Maleficent had a lot of lines, just like Uncle Jay had said. I wasn't sure how I was going to mem-orize all of them by next week), I sort of found myself imitating Erica's sister Missy. Just a little. This, I noticed, made Rosemary, Sophie and Caroline laugh. A lot. Even Erica tittered a little once in a while.

Soon other people in the class started laughing too . . . although they didn't know who I was imitating. Even Mrs Hunter laughed. But she looked like she was trying not to. The corners of her mouth were twitching as she said, 'That's very nice, Allie.'

Making people laugh – especially when they don't want to – is a really nice feeling, it turns out. I don't know for sure – only Sophie can say – but I think it *might* be an even better feeling than playing a princess.

It started to dawn on me that maybe I had been looking at this evil-queen thing all wrong. Maybe I shouldn't be mad I wasn't getting to play the beautiful princess, but happy I was getting to play a part that could, potentially, make people laugh.

Except . . . wasn't the evil queen supposed to be scary? See, that was the problem: I just didn't know for sure. I was still confused about the whole thing. I knew this was part of the whole 'motivation' thing Uncle Jay had been talking about. I *had* to figure out what happened in Queen Melissa the Maleficent's life to have made her so evil in the first place! Why did she drink so many boxes of juice and just toss them into the garbage instead of the recycling bin, and drive such a big, gas-guzzling car such short distances that she could easily have walked? Why had she bought a pollution ray with which to kill Princess Penelope in the first place?

These were the things I knew I still had to figure out about her, in order to really get to know my character, as Uncle Jay would say . . .

But I figured I had plenty of time before the big performance.

It was as we were going out for recess towards the end of the week that an interesting thing happened. And that's how I knew for sure why Cheyenne always sounded so boring when she was saying her lines as the fairy queen. She was doing it on purpose!

'I mean,' I overheard Cheyenne saying to Elizabeth

Pukowski, who played a public-transportation elf, 'Mrs Hunter can force me to play the fairy queen, but she can't force me to play her *well*.'

I elbowed Sophie. Sophie grabbed her side and made a face as if I'd really hurt her (I hadn't). I nodded my head meaningfully towards the girls in front of us and indicated that Sophie should listen to what they were saying.

'What do you mean?' Elizabeth looked at Shamira, who also played a public-transportation elf.

'Well, I'll play the fairy queen,' Cheyenne said with her nose in the air, 'but I'm not going to put any *emotional investment* into it. I mean, why should I? It's just a silly children's play. I'm going to save my most powerful acting for my next audition, whatever it is. Why waste my energy on this stupid play, which only our parents are going to see?'

Elizabeth and Shamira looked at one another.

'I don't want to do a bad job in front of my mom and dad,' Shamira said.

'But that's just it,' Cheyenne said. 'My parents know the kind of acting I'm capable of. I played Helen Keller, after all. Talent like mine is wasted in a part like this. So why put myself out there, is all I'm saying? "M and D" agree.'

Marianne and Dominique, who'd been trailing

along behind Cheyenne, but in front of Sophie and me, both nodded.

'So,' Sophie interrupted, unable to control herself a second longer, she was so mad. 'You're not even going to *try* to be good in the play?'

'No,' Cheyenne said with a shrug. She didn't look ashamed of herself or anything.

'But . . .' Sophie looked stunned. 'You *have* to.'

'No,' Cheyenne said. 'I don't.'

Sophie's eyes seemed to glaze over, and for a second I thought her head might spin off her body.

'Yes you do, Cheyenne,' she practically screamed. 'You have to try! Because it's a play, and I'm the star of it, and I said so! Everyone has to do their best in it!'

Whoa. Sophie had maybe let her starring role go to her head a bit.

I laid a gentle hand on her shoulder and patted it a little, trying to get her to calm down. To Cheyenne, who was smirking at Sophie's outburst, I said, 'That's a really bad attitude, Cheyenne. Just because you don't like the part you got. There are no small parts, you know. Only small actors.'

Cheyenne stopped smirking at Sophie and looked at me all bug-eyed. 'What does that even mean?' she wanted to know.

'Figure it out,' I advised her. And then I took a seething Sophie's arm and steered her away from them.

'Oh,' Sophie fretted, when we joined Caroline and Erica at our special area where we played queens, 'I just can't believe her! She's so horrible! I thought things were going to get better the more we rehearsed, but now I know they're not. The play is going to be awful!'

'No,' Caroline said calmly, after I'd explained what Sophie was talking about. 'Cheyenne and those guys will be awful. *We* will still be good.'

'You know what I mean,' Sophie said. She slumped down on to the grass. 'What are we going to do?'

'Maybe we should tell Mrs Hunter,' Erica said, looking concerned.

'Yeah!' Sophie brightened. 'Let's tell Mrs Hunter! That's a great idea!'

I eyed Sophie a little worriedly. Yeah, the Princess Penelope thing had definitely gone to her head.

'That will only get them more mad,' Caroline said. 'Honestly, I don't think there's anything we *can* do. *You can't make someone with a bad attitude about something change their mind and have a good one. You just can't.*'

That sounded like a rule to me.

A rule that was made to be broken.

The only problem was, I had no idea how to go about breaking it.

Cheyenne and her compact-fluorescent-bulb fairy court not even trying to act when it came time to say their lines wasn't my only problem, though. Sophie maybe letting playing a princess go to her head wasn't either. The fact was, I still didn't feel as if I had pinned down my character's motivation. What had happened to Queen Melissa the Maleficent in her life that had made her choose to be the way she was – evil?

Because everyone knew the way to get friends was to *Treat people the way you yourself would like to be treated*. That's the number one rule of all!

And OK, in my experience not very many people actually follow that rule. But you're *supposed* to.

So what kind of person would pick being mean all the time over being nice?

I knew there was only one person I could turn to with all my theatre-related problems. And fortunately he came over that night, because Mom's second segment on *Good News!* was going to be on. Uncle Jay and Harmony brought over pizza from Pizza Express, and also Dairy Queen for dessert for us, in honour of the special occasion (and we had all promised not to spill, even though of course Mark had already dribbled a huge portion of his vanilla twist cherry dip down his front).

'Tonight on *Good News!*,' Lynn Martinez said on the television we were all sitting in front of, 'our weekly movie commentator Elizabeth Finkle takes us to the movies and tells us what she thinks about this week's latest indie release, *Interlude with Rasputin*.'

Then Mom's head filled the screen.

Only . . . she looked really different than she had last week. At first I couldn't figure out how. Then I did.

'Hey, Mom,' I said. 'What did you do to your eyes?'

'Why?' Mom asked. 'Do you like them?'

'Yes,' I said. 'They look really good. I mean, they always look good. But—'

'They look gigantic,' Mark said.

'Like there are spiders crawling out of them,' Kevin said.

'In a good way,' Uncle Jay said, really fast.

Mom looked up at Dad, who was smiling.

'You do look great, Liz,' Dad said.

'I bought false eyelashes,' Mom said. 'The lights from the studio wash out my own eyelashes, because they're so fair, so I just put on false ones. They really work, don't they?'

'Do they ever,' Harmony said. 'Did Lynn Martinez give you that tip?'

'As a matter of fact,' Mom said, 'she did.'

Mom gave *Interlude with Rasputin* a big thumbs down. She said it wasn't quite the moving triumph of the human spirit the movie poster promised it would be. She said it was more like a moving triumph of bad movie making. She told everyone to save their money for the new Taylor Swift movie that was coming out next weekend.

I knew with a recommendation like that I was sure to be even more popular with the fifth-grade girls! Maybe they'd crown me queen of the fourth-graders, or something.

It was after Mom had shown Harmony and me how her false eyelashes worked (easy: you just peel them from their case and stick them on over your real eyelashes. They're self-adhesive) that I went back out into the kitchen to fill the dishwasher (because it was my turn) and Uncle Jay asked me how rehearsals for *Princess Penelope in the Realm of Recycling* were going.

'Not so good,' I said with a sigh. Then I told him about how I was having trouble coming up with a reason for my character to be so mean to everyone, and also about how Cheyenne and 'M and D' refused to act, and how Sophie was acting like such a princess about it.

'And I guess I can't really blame her,' I said to him. 'It's like they don't even care whether or not the play is any good.'

'Well,' Uncle Jay said, 'you didn't used to care either, remember? Back when you were so disappointed about not getting the part of Princess Penelope. What changed your mind?'

Uncle Jay was right! I hadn't cared about the play back then.

And I *was* still sad about not getting to wear my gold flower-girl dress and be the star and not getting to come to school in a limo (although that could still happen. There was still a chance Mom could become a star, and me the child of a star).

But I wasn't as upset about not getting the part as I had been before.

And a lot of that, I had to admit, was because of how good Sophie had made me feel when she'd come back to rescue me when Missy had been holding me captive.

But another part of it was how much everybody had been laughing when I'd been saying my lines as Queen Melissa the Maleficent. It felt really good to make people laugh – and to know that people liked me.

'Maybe,' I said slowly, 'we just need to tell them how good they are as compact-fluorescent-bulb fairies?'

'Maybe you do,' Uncle Jay said. 'Maybe it's as simple as paying them some attention. Sometimes a little positive reinforcement is all people need. Like with Mewsie. You don't punish him when he's being bad.'

'No!' I said, shocked. 'I reward him when he's being good!'

'Exactly,' Uncle Jay said. 'Why don't you try that with the fairy girls? They must do good things sometimes.'

I tried to think if Cheyenne and her friends had ever done anything remotely nice. But I really couldn't think of anything.

'Well,' I said after I'd given up, 'I guess we could just lie, and give them positive reinforcement for nothing.'

'That'll work too,' Uncle Jay said. 'And as for your character's motivation, I don't think I can help you. Developing one's character is a deeply personal experience, and it would be wrong for me to get involved. You keep working on it. I'm sure inspiration will strike soon.'

I wasn't as sure about that as Uncle Jay was, though I had no choice but to go along with it. Just like, when I got to the Stop sign the next morning, I had to tell Caroline, Sophie and Erica that from now on we were going to tell Cheyenne, Dominique and Marianne what a good job they were doing as fairies.

Sophie looked at me like I was crazy. 'But they're *horrible* fairies. They're acting horrible *on purpose*. Remember? They admitted it to our faces.'

'I know,' I said. 'But if we tell them how good we think they are, maybe they'll start acting better. It's called positive reinforcement. And the thing is, they can't start acting any *worse*.'

'Well,' Caroline said, looking thoughtful, 'that's true.'

'You mean you want us to lie?' Erica looked scared. Erica doesn't like lying, even when it's to make someone else feel better. I've tried to explain to Erica that this kind of lying is OK, but it still makes her uncomfortable. I've even been tempted to show Erica my book of rules, where *It's OK to lie if the lie makes someone else feel better* is totally on the list.

But things didn't turn out so well last time I showed someone my book of rules, so it's probably best if I just keep it to myself.

'It's just a little lie,' I told her. 'For the good of the play.'

'Then I think we should do it,' Sophie said. 'For the good of the play.' Since she had the lead in the play, it made sense that she would think this, of course.

'It can't hurt,' Caroline said. 'And the real danger we want to avoid is, now that the other girls, like Elizabeth and Shamira, know what Cheyenne and those guys are doing, acting horrible on purpose, they might start acting horrible too.'

Sophie gasped. 'No! You don't think they'd—'

'Yeah,' Caroline said grimly, 'I do. And that would be awful. Soon everyone in the whole play, except for us, might start acting horrible on purpose. So Allie's right. This is our only plan. We have to do *something*.'

'I think you guys should do it,' Kevin said.

'Kevin's right,' Sophie said with a sigh. 'Let's pretend we think they're good, and tell them so. Deal?' Sophie held up her hand for a fist bump.

'Deal,' I said, and held up my own fist.

'Deal,' Caroline said, and held up hers.

'Deal,' Kevin said, and put up his fist as well.

We all looked inquiringly at Erica. Finally she said, 'Oh, all right. But it's going to feel so wrong to lie, you guys!' and bumped her fist against each of ours.

In the afternoons, we didn't have rehearsals. We had set building. We were constructing cardboard trees (to be part of the forest Princess Penelope wanders into when she gets to the Realm of Recycling) and the walls of the Castle of Plastic Doom (Queen

Melissa the Maleficent lived in the castle, where she watched everything that was happening to Princess Penelope through her crystal computer monitor) as well as things like a papier-mâché cave for Lenny the recycled-paper dragon to live in and stuff.

Different people were in charge of different parts of the set construction – mainly based on what they liked doing. Caroline, Joey Fields and Elizabeth Pukowski got to do all the papier mâché, because they liked dipping strips of paper into glue and getting their hands all messy. Stuart, Sophie, Shamira, Lenny and I did all the painting, because we were all a little artistic and liked drawing and colouring. Patrick Day, Rosemary and Mrs Hunter were in charge of the hot-glue guns for making the cardboard trees and castle walls, because Patrick and Rosemary liked guns, and Mrs Hunter liked supervising them.

Cheyenne and her fairy court (Marianne and Dominique) appointed themselves in charge of putting sparkles on everything. For some reason they thought the Realm of Recycling should be sparkly. So Mrs Hunter brought them tons of glitter from the craft store, and Cheyenne and 'M and D' went around throwing handfuls of it everywhere. Even on places it didn't really go, like Lenny's dragon cave and the evil queen's computer monitor.

I have to admit, I found their 'fairy-dust sprinkling' kind of annoying, especially when I got home and pulled off my cowboy boots and a bunch of glitter came pouring out of them on to my bedroom carpet.

But since we'd agreed to start complimenting the fairy queen and her court in an effort to get them more into the spirit of the play, I started going, 'That looks really good,' to them every time they threw glitter on something.

At first they would just give me funny looks. But then Dominique went, 'Uh . . . thanks.'

Marianne was the one who seemed to be getting over not having won the part of Princess Penelope the fastest. When I complimented her glitter-throwing technique, she said, 'Thanks! It does look good, doesn't it?' all brightly.

It was working! Our complimenting them was starting to put them in a better mood about the play!

Well, some of them.

Because when I said, 'That's looking really pretty,' to Cheyenne about the cardboard toadstool she was glitterfying, she looked up at me sourly from where she was kneeling and went, 'Shut up.'

I didn't think I'd heard her right. I said, 'Excuse me?'

'I said shut up.' Cheyenne went back to sprinkling glitter.

I felt my face turning red. I couldn't believe it! Cheyenne had told me to shut up, exactly the way she'd told her mom to shut up back at the mall that day I'd been spying on them both in the earring section!

And just like Cheyenne's mom, all I'd done was try to be nice to her!

Then I remembered something: Evil Queen Melissa the Maleficent tried through the whole play to have Princess Penelope killed . . .

. . . and all Princess Penelope had ever done to her was be nice to her!

And suddenly, just like Uncle Jay had said it would, inspiration struck.

I had my motivation for the character of the evil queen.

Cheyenne O'Malley, the most evil girl I had ever met!

Rule #11

Make the Best of It

Rehearsals were going really well. At least in my opinion. I had all my lines memorized by the second week. The secret to memorizing lines, it turns out, is practice. I just practised my lines all the time. Like at night, right before I'd fall asleep. And in my head in the morning, while I was brushing my teeth. It was easy to memorize my lines by thinking about them at night, in the morning, and then saying them out loud at rehearsal.

Some people, though, weren't having as easy a time of it. Like Patrick Day. He only had one line – 'There she is! Now we will smite her with the pollution ray!' – but he couldn't seem to remember it. The names and makes of the kinds of cars he wanted to drive when he was old enough for a licence? No problem. But that line? Forget about it. His fellow soldier, Rosemary, was always having to whisper it to him.

STAGE FRIGHT

Some people, I guess, aren't made for a life on the stage.

That wasn't the only ongoing problem with Room 209's production for the open house. Another one was that I had been totally right about Cheyenne: she really was evil. Even though Dominique and Marianne had finally started acting, Cheyenne still refused, and said her lines like a robot. We were all complimenting her performances like crazy, but she only turned up her nose at us. And I wasn't the only one who noticed that, whenever Sophie said a line, Cheyenne mouthed it along with her.

'She's memorized all the princess's lines!' Rosemary whispered one morning during rehearsal, when we were watching Sophie perform a scene we weren't in. Cheyenne wasn't in it either, and was sitting on the side of the stage with us.

'She must think if Sophie gets sick or something, she's going to get asked by Mrs Hunter to take over the part!' Rosemary whispered in disgust.

I nodded but didn't say anything. Because the thing was, I had sort of memorized all Princess Penelope's lines too, in case the same thing happened. I mean, Sophie does get sick a lot. I overheard my mom tell my dad that she thinks Sophie's a little bit of a hypochondriac, which means someone who always thinks she's coming down with something, but who never actually gets really sick.

But I wasn't hoping something bad would happen to Sophie and that I'd have to step into the part of Princess Penelope in her absence . . . even though I was totally prepared to do so in the event that this happened. I didn't really want Sophie to get sick. I couldn't help memorizing the princess's lines. I'd just heard them so many times, they sort of stuck in my head.

Cheyenne though, you could tell, was totally hoping something would happen to Sophie. Talk about evil!

Cheyenne wasn't the only one who seemed to have Sophie on the brain.

'Have you guys noticed that Joey Fields has been acting weird lately?' Sophie asked, one day on our way down to morning recess.

'He's been barking less than usual,' I said.

I should know, since I have to sit next to him all day. Joey has this thing where sometimes he barks and growls like a dog instead of talking. But using Uncle Jay's theory of positive reinforcement, I've been rewarding him by not flicking him with rubber bands when he isn't doing it, and as a consequence he'd been doing it a lot less.

'I don't mean that,' Sophie said. 'I mean, he keeps coming up to me at rehearsal and asking me weird questions. Like if I like candy bars, and what kind. Does he do that to you?'

'If he did,' Rosemary said, 'I'd stuff him in a folding chair.'

'It sounds like he likes you,' Caroline said, ignoring Rosemary.

I was surprised to hear this about Joey – that he might like Sophie. A little while ago, Joey had liked me and had asked me to go with him, even though I had said no. How could he have suddenly switched to liking Sophie? True, he did play the kindly wizard who tries to help Princess Penelope understand about wasteful plastic-water-bottle usage and find her way to her fairy godmother's house through the Realm of Recycling, and so he had a scene with her in the play.

And true, I didn't like him in that way.

But it was kind of messed up of him to just go around switching liking girls like that, every other month. Boys are so weird.

'Ew,' Sophie said. 'I hope he doesn't like me. I don't like him.'

'Oh,' Erica said, sounding upset, 'Joey's nice. At least, he's nicer than all the other boys. Except Lenny Hsu. Joey doesn't throw things, or make rude noises when the principal walks by.'

'Ew,' Sophie said again. She was obviously still thinking about Joey liking her.

This was the thing about getting to be the star of the play. All the boys – well, Joey Fields anyway – fell in love with you. Not that this was something you necessarily wanted, because to tell the truth I've been there with Joey, and it's not actually all that great.

But still. No one falls in love with the evil queen. *No one.*

And no one memorizes the evil queen's lines in the hopes that she'll get sick and they can take over her part. *No one.*

But Queen Melissa the Maleficent was my part, and I was going to make the best of her. Because that's what you do in a bad situation. *Make the best of it.* That's a rule.

So on the day of Room 209's open house, when we were having our first dress rehearsal in the morning, and I brought in my costume that I'd assembled from stuff I'd found in my closet, plus the dress my mom had loaned me and Dad's Dracula cape, I wasn't prepared for the amount of criticism I received because of it.

Because I really thought my costume looked good. Sure, it wasn't one of the costumes the parents of the elves and soldiers had all gotten together to hand sew so they'd all look the same. My mom had asked me if I'd wanted help and I'd said no, that I'd put my costume together myself.

But that didn't make it a bad costume. I thought it looked good.

But Sophie didn't seem to like it. She seemed kind of mad about it, as a matter of fact.

'But,' she said when I came out of the girls' room, where we'd all gone to change before rehearsal. 'You're supposed to be *evil*. An *evil* queen.'

'I *am* evil,' I said, looking down at myself.

'But –' Sophie glanced over at Erica, Caroline and Rosemary, as if for support. Only I didn't think she was going to get any from Rosemary, since Rosemary was laughing too hard. She'd started laughing the minute I came out of the cubicle. And she couldn't seem to stop – 'I don't think an evil queen would wear red high-tops,' Sophie said. 'And those striped socks.'

I looked down at my shoes. I'd thought very carefully about my character.

But I'd also thought about the audience we were going to have at the open house. And the fact that there'd be little kids there. Some of them, the little brothers and sisters of kids in our class and Mrs Danielson's class, would be even younger than Kevin. I didn't want Queen Melissa the Maleficent to be *too* scary.

'I think the evil queen would wear these shoes,' I said to Sophie.

'Well,' Sophie said in a snippy voice, 'I don't think she would. I think she would wear something more glamorous. Also, more evil.'

'Well,' I said, 'I don't know what evil shoes look like. Also, she's my character, and I say she would wear these shoes. You can dress up your character however you want, but mine wears red high-tops. And striped socks.'

Sophie looked like she was about to argue some more, but Erica broke in, waving her fairy-godmother wand and going, 'You guys, let's not fight. I think you both look beautiful.'

And Caroline said quickly, when Sophie drew in a deep breath to argue some more, 'Yeah, let's let Mrs Hunter decide. She's the director, after all. If she doesn't like Allie's costume, Sophie, she'll say something.'

Sophie looked doubtful but kept her mouth shut.

Until she saw Cheyenne's costume.

'Wh-what,' Sophie stammered, pointing across the classroom when we all walked back into it, 'is *she* wearing?'

We soon found out. You could hear Cheyenne bragging away from down the hall practically. She'd gotten her mom to find her an actual store-bought fairy costume (everyone else's was homemade).

'She ordered it from a costume shop on the Internet,' Cheyenne said, smoothing the sparkling, multilayered skirt of her gown. Cheyenne said it was made of something called 'tulle'. 'All the way from New York City.'

'M and D' and all the other girls in Room 209 admired Cheyenne's specially ordered costume and went, 'Ooooh.'

Sophie looked down at her own costume – which her mother had gotten her at Good Will (it was someone's old prom dress), and which if you asked me was perfectly nice – and went, 'But . . . her costume is nicer than mine!'

'Your costume is very pretty, Sophie,' Erica said.

'No it's not,' Sophie said. 'Look at Cheyenne's! It's way sparklier!'

'Well, Cheyenne's a fairy queen,' Caroline pointed out. 'You're just a princess.'

'But –' I wouldn't have believed it if I hadn't seen it with my own eyes, but Sophie looked as if she was about to cry – 'I'm the star!'

Oh, brother.

'Sophie,' I said, 'Princess Penelope isn't supposed

to look that great anyway. Remember? Her evil stepmother has just thrown her out of the Castle of
Plastic Doom. She's been wandering around the
Realm of Recycling for days. It makes sense that her
dress wouldn't be in such terrific shape. Not,' I hurried to add, when I saw her trembling lower lip, 'that
yours isn't totally pretty.'

Sophie was still staring over at Cheyenne. 'Look at
her tiara!'

It was true. Cheyenne's tiara was pretty great. It
looked like something the Sugar Plum Fairy would
have worn in *The Nutcracker* – if the Sugar Plum
Fairy had worn a crown with compact fluorescent
bulbs sticking out of the top of it.

Still, Cheyenne's fairy crown put Sophie's crown
and my crown, which were plastic and left over from
birthday parties, to shame. Cheyenne's crown was
like two feet tall (not counting the light bulbs) with
crystals dangling off the top, like the ones from Brittany Hauser's mom's dining-room chandelier.

Cheyenne also had real fairy wings that were
almost as big as her, dripping in fairy dust and not
droopy like Erica's, which were borrowed from Missy
from when she'd dressed as an angel one Halloween.

'It's not fair,' Sophie said, her eyebrows beginning
to slant downwards angrily. '*I'm* the star of the play. *I*

should have the nicest costume. Cheyenne totally did this on purpose, to make me look bad.'

'Oh, I don't think she did it on purpose,' Erica said, looking distressed.

'I'm going to march over there,' Sophie said, 'and give her a piece of my—'

Fortunately, at that moment, Mrs Hunter came into Room 209, clapped her hands and said, 'Class, I have an exciting announcement to make. For our first dress rehearsal, we're actually going to have an audience. The morning kindergarten class is going to come in to watch our performance. Isn't that exciting? So let's try to put on an extra-good show. OK? So, places everybody!'

This was fantastic! We were going to be doing our show in front of actual human beings for the first time!

And, OK, one of them was going to be Kevin. But that was all right.

'Oh,' Erica cried, 'I'm so nervous!'

'It'll be OK,' I said. Although the truth was, I was nervous now too. What if Sophie was right, and my red high-tops were all wrong for the part?

We all filed downstairs to the auditorium and went backstage, where I immediately had to break up a cardboard sword-fight between Patrick Day and

Stuart Maxwell, then show Patrick how to write his line down on his sword so he wouldn't forget it.

That's when we heard all the kindergarteners coming in. It was hard not to start feeling even more nervous. Although they were just kindergarteners, we still wanted to put on a good show for them. At least, I did.

'Oh my goodness –' Sophie looked especially delicate in the dark shadows backstage – 'I think I'm going to be sick. Do I feel feverish to you?'

'If you need to go to the nurse's office,' Cheyenne whispered as Erica felt Sophie's forehead to see if it was hot, 'I can take over your part.'

'No,' Sophie said, eyeing Cheyenne with distaste. 'I'll be fine, thanks, Cheyenne.'

Then Sophie turned to me and asked, sounding a little annoyed, 'Allie, you're not *really* going out in those shoes, are you?'

I looked down at my red high-tops.

'Yeah,' I said, 'I am. Why?'

'I just really don't think they're right for the part.' Sophie seemed upset. 'They're so . . .'

But Sophie never got to finish what she was going to say. Because it was time for the play to begin!

Princess Penelope had the first few lines (about her dad dying). Then I came on. I waited in the wings, which is the backstage area, for my cue, which is the line Sophie was supposed to say that was my signal to come out on stage. I could see all the kindergarteners sitting on the floor of the auditorium slash gym slash cafeteria, looking up at the stage. I couldn't see Kevin though. My heart was beating kind of hard, even though I told myself it didn't matter, because it was just kindergarteners. But it still mattered, because I wanted to do a good job. Why didn't Cheyenne see it that way?

Then Sophie said my cue and I felt a huge swoop of nervousness come up from my stomach and into my throat. I thought I might even be having a heart attack.

Then I remembered I wasn't supposed to be me, Allie Finkle, any more. I was supposed to be Queen Melissa the Maleficent, who hated recycling and hated Princess Penelope even more. *She* would never be nervous about speaking in front of kindergarteners, or anyone really. Because she was a queen.

So I went out on stage, using my big loud evil-queen voice.

And everyone started laughing. I could hear Kevin laughing loudest of all. I could see him sitting in the midst of all the kindergarteners, laughing his head off and pointing at me, going, 'That's her! That's my sister!'

And I stopped being nervous and started having fun being Queen Melissa, the spoilt, bratty queen who was used to getting everything her way, because her mother always gave her every single thing she ever wanted, even the amethyst earrings she saw in the mall and just wanted on a whim. No one ever said no to her, even when she was rude and told her own mother to *shut up*.

And that's why she's so evil. She just didn't know better really.

But the thing was, Cheyenne didn't even notice I was basing my performance on her! I knew she didn't notice, because she didn't say anything about it to me. In fact, Cheyenne was so caught up in showing off in her fabulous costume, she even forgot about pretending she didn't know how to act. She put on a fantastic performance as the compact-fluorescent-bulb fairy queen for the kindergarteners. She didn't do her robot voice, and even pirouetted around the stage a little in her fancy pink fairy slippers (some of the kindergartener girls actually gasped when Cheyenne came out on stage, she looked so pretty, which I'm sure helped her ego a little). She tossed her bouncy hair and flitted around, shaking her wings. She was perfect!

In fact, *everyone* was perfect. Patrick didn't forget his line (he read it off his sword), and Caroline pranced perfectly (her unicorn horn didn't fall off once), and Erica was a perfect motherly fairy godmother. I got tons of laughs and applause during my big death scene, which I stretched out as long as possible, dying in the most dramatic way I knew how. I even heard the boys from Room 209 laughing backstage. I made sure when I was dead that my mom's dress was pulled up so my striped socks and red high-tops showed.

That got the biggest laugh of all from the kindergarteners. Also, a big cheer.

Which meant I had done a good job. Because if people aren't happy when the bad guy dies, it means the character actor playing the bad guy didn't play the bad guy right.

When the performance was over and we all came out to take our bows, the kindergarteners actually stood up to clap!

And OK, they're just kindergarteners . . .

But that was a good sign that our play didn't stink. Which was good because we had worked really hard on it.

I was super excited about the kindergarteners loving our play. So were Erica and Caroline and Rosemary. We were jumping around the stage, hugging each other, along with Elizabeth Pukowski and Shamira and some other girls. Which was why I was kind of surprised when Sophie turned to me when I tried to hug her and said in an angry voice, 'Get away from me, Allie. Don't you know you ruined the whole play?'

Really, nothing could have shocked me more. Unless maybe Sophie had told me she was leaving Pine Heights Elementary School to go star with the Jonas Brothers in their next movie.

'What?' I looked around all shocked, to see if anyone else felt this way. But Erica and Caroline and Rosemary and everyone just looked back at me blankly, as confused as I was.

'How did I ruin the whole play?' I asked.

'With those shoes,' Sophie said, pointing accusingly at my high-tops. 'When you came out on stage, everyone laughed!'

I knew everyone had laughed when I came out on stage. I'd *wanted* everyone to laugh at my costume. That had been my intention. Hearing them laugh like that had felt good.

'It's nice to make people laugh, Sophie,' I said. I didn't understand why she was so mad.

'But the evil queen is supposed to be *evil*,' Sophie said. 'That's why she's called the evil queen! You're supposed to be scary, not funny. And when you die, it's not supposed to be funny. But everyone laughed! They laughed! And at the end, people clapped more for you than they did for me! But I'm supposed to be the star! Princess Penelope!'

I looked over from Sophie to Caroline, who gave

me a shrug. She didn't know what to make of Sophie's temper tantrum either. Neither, I could tell, did Erica. Or Rosemary.

I didn't know what to do. Or say. I could tell Sophie was upset.

But if you asked me, she was acting a little bit like a spoilt princess.

'I'm sorry, Sophie,' I said, 'but people didn't clap more for me than they did for you—'

'Yes they did!' Sophie yelled. 'They did!'

'That's because Allie's brother was in the audience, Sophie,' Caroline explained. 'That's all.'

Sophie made fists out of both her hands, rolled her eyes and yelled, 'I'm the star of this play, Allie! *Me!* Not *you!* Why won't anyone remember that? Ugh, *I hate you!*'

The unfortunate part for Sophie, though, was that she yelled this right in front of Mrs Hunter, who'd come up to see what all the yelling was about.

Mrs Hunter, looking very shocked, cried, 'Sophie Abramowitz! Come see me in the hallway immediately, please.'

Sophie, the minute she heard Mrs Hunter's voice, looked very sorry for her outburst. Her cheeks began to burn bright red, and her eyes filled with tears as she slowly climbed down from the stage to follow Mrs Hunter from the gym.

'This,' I said, looking down at my high-tops and feeling a big lump forming in my throat, 'is all my fault.'

'No it's not,' said Erica. 'I'm sure Sophie only said that because she's super nervous about the big performance tonight. Mrs Hunter will have a talk with her and everything will be all right. You'll see.'

Except it wasn't. Because when Sophie got back from her talk with Mrs Hunter, she was crying hysterically.

'You g-guys,' she said, wiping her tears away with the back of her wrist. 'Mrs Hunter says I c-can't play Princess Penelope t-tonight! I'm out of the p-play!'

Rule #12

When You Know the
Right Thing to Do, You
Have to Do It

So. It was all up to me.

I'd always known that it would be in the end.

Well, Mrs Hunter didn't have to worry. I was ready. I knew all Princess Penelope's lines, and her blocking. I was completely prepared to step into her part. I even had a costume – my gold flower-girl dress. I would wear it with my black patent-leather party shoes (if they still fitted . . . I hadn't tried them on in a while).

Of course, there was the small question of who would play the part of the evil queen.

But I even had an answer ready for that: Mrs Hunter, of course. Mrs Hunter could play the evil queen herself. There was no reason why she shouldn't. She wasn't doing anything during the performance anyway, except running around making sure we had our props, like Erica's reusable-cloth shopping bags and such, and seeing that we got on to the stage on time, and opening and closing the curtains.

But Mrs Jenkins could do all that. She was the principal, after all.

And yes, I did feel bad for Sophie. Of course I did.

But she had made her own misfortune by letting her celebrity go to her head. I mean, my mother was the star of a local cable television programme, but had I let that go to my head, and become super bossy and started telling my friends that I hated them? No.

Sophie really had no one to blame but herself.

'But has Mrs Hunter *asked* you to take over Sophie's part?' Mom inquired that day at lunch. Because I'd brought down my flower-girl dress for her to iron, assuring her I was going to be needing it that night at the open house.

'Well,' I said, 'not officially. But I'm positive she's going to.'

'Oh, honey.' Mom took the dress from me. 'If she hasn't asked you, I really don't think you should get your hopes up.'

'But, Mom,' I said. 'There's no one else she *can* ask. Cheyenne has been acting horribly lately. There's no way Mrs Hunter is going to ask *her* to play Princess Penelope. And I'm the next best actress in the whole class. I mean, not to be a braggart or anything.'

'She really is good, Mom,' Kevin chimed in from the kitchen counter, where he was eating grilled cheese. 'You should see her. She was awesome.'

'Well, I hope you're right,' Mom said. 'Because I hate to see you disappointed. And your father was really looking forward to seeing you in his Dracula cape.'

'This will be much better,' I assured her. 'You'll see.'

It had been hard walking a sobbing Sophie home for lunch. Mainly because I'd been waiting for her to apologize for saying she hated me, only she hadn't. Not even once. Possibly because she'd been crying so hard over losing the part of Princess Penelope. Still, you would have thought she'd stop to think about *my* feelings for a change.

We'd tried to support her as best we could, telling her that maybe Mrs Hunter would change her mind.

But of course I for one didn't really believe that. I suspected Sophie had been rehearsing the part of Princess Penelope so much that she had actually temporarily turned into a princess herself, and thought she could start telling other people what to do (like me with my shoes for my evil-queen costume), and she'd failed to remember the number-one rule – treat people the way you yourself would like to be treated (because of the way she'd told me that she hated me).

Especially since she refused even to consider apologizing to me. She kept saying she thought Mrs Hunter should apologize to *her* for taking her out of the play.

She never even *mentioned* apologizing to me.

Oh yes. The part of Princess Penelope was going to be mine all right.

Erica was really worried about Sophie – especially when we were walking back to school after lunch, and Caroline appeared all alone at the Stop sign where we usually met to walk to Pine Heights together.

'Sophie's mom says she made herself too sick from crying to come back to school,' Caroline explained worriedly. 'So she has a stomach ache and is going to stay home for the rest of the day.'

'Oh no!' Erica cried. 'That's terrible.'

'Well,' I said philosophically, 'Sophie brought it on herself. She should have apologized to all of us for being so bossy.' I didn't mention that she should have apologized to me for saying she hated me. That seemed like it should have been a given.

'Yes,' Caroline said, 'but don't you think the whole thing was only nerves about tonight?'

'Or maybe she thinks she really is a princess,' I said.

'Come on,' Caroline said. 'Sophie doesn't think she really is a princess.'

'Then why was she telling me what to do with my

own costume?' I asked. 'And why did she say she hated me?'

'Well,' Caroline said, 'maybe taking the afternoon off will give her a chance to cool down.'

Maybe it would. But maybe it would also be too late for her to get the part of Princess Penelope back.

Because maybe it was mine now.

What if Mom invited Lynn Martinez from *Good News!* to the show tonight to see me? They were such good friends now, on account of sharing that tip about false eyelashes, she probably would.

And if Lynn saw me as Princess Penelope, she would probably ask me to come on her show so she could interview me. And then a talent scout from Hollywood would see me, and ask me to star in my own reality show about a fourth-grade animal-lover with two pesky little brothers whose mother is also a TV star.

The only problem with this plan was, when we got back to school, Cheyenne was going around saying Mrs Hunter was going to ask *her* to play Princess Penelope.

'Naturally,' Cheyenne said, loudly enough for all of us to hear her over by the swings, where we were standing. 'I mean, who else would she ask at the last minute, but the one *semi-professional* actress she has in her class?'

'But what about your fairy-queen costume?'

Dominique asked her. 'You said your mom spent over two hundred dollars on it.'

'It can easily be converted into a princess costume,' Cheyenne said. 'Simply by removing the wings.'

'Oh!' Erica said when she overheard all this. 'Do you believe them? Talking about taking over Sophie's part like she's dead or something. You know, Mrs Hunter would probably still give the part back to Sophie, if she'd just apologize to Allie.'

I didn't want to tell Erica she was wrong straight to her face. First of all, I for one didn't plan on forgiving Sophie that easily. And second of all, I didn't want to get her hopes up, either.

'Well, it's good to make alternative plans,' I said. 'I mean, just in case Sophie doesn't come back.'

'But you don't really think Mrs Hunter would give the part of Princess Penelope to Cheyenne, do you?' Erica looked worried.

'Probably not,' I said. 'I think Mrs Hunter would probably give the part to the next best person who auditioned for it.'

Erica thought about that. 'Well, Marianne and Dominique weren't very good. And I can't imagine her giving it to Elizabeth or one of the other elves . . . and Caroline, you wouldn't want it, would you?'

'No way. I love being a unicorn. But who else . . .'

Then I caught Caroline looking at me. 'Allie. Would *you* want it?'

Erica's eyes widened. 'Allie? Really? Do you know all Sophie's lines?'

'Sure,' I said, shrugging modestly. 'Memorizing lines is easy.'

'But then . . .' Erica looked stunned. 'Who would play the evil queen?'

'Mrs Hunter, I guess,' I said, with another shrug.

'But you're so good as the evil queen,' Erica cried. 'We love you as the evil queen. You make us laugh!'

I stared at her. 'Really?' I knew I made Mrs Hunter laugh. And my little brother. And the boys. But not the rest of the class.

'Really,' Erica said. 'Oh, you can't not play the evil queen. You're so good at playing her! The play won't be as good without you!'

I had never considered this before – that I was so good at playing the evil queen, the play might not be as good if I played Princess Penelope instead. I had wanted to play Princess Penelope so badly, that was all I had ever really thought about.

'It really would be a shame,' Caroline said. 'I don't think Mrs Hunter would be as good as you are at playing the evil queen.'

'Well,' I said. I looked down at my feet. I was still

wearing my red high-tops. It had been too much trouble to take them off after rehearsal . . . although it had occurred to me if I was going to be playing Princess Penelope that night, I'd have to take them off anyway. Unless I decided Princess Penelope was the type of character who would wear high-tops. You never knew. As I portrayed her, she might be. 'I guess we'll see how it goes.'

When we got into Room 209 after lunch-break, the mood of the class was sombre. You could tell everyone had noticed Sophie hadn't come back from lunch.

'Well, class,' Mrs Hunter said, coming to the front of the room, 'as Sophie Abramowitz won't be performing tonight as Princess Penelope, we're going to need to replace her part. Is there anyone here who thinks they know her lines well enough to—'

Even before the words were all the way out of Mrs Hunter's mouth, Cheyenne's hand shot up into the air. Not to let her have the advantage, I put my hand in the air too. Mrs Hunter looked at both of us.

'Cheyenne and Allie, you both think you know all Princess Penelope's lines?'

Cheyenne put her hand down and turned in her chair to look at me. I would not be exaggerating if I said she was giving me the stare of death.

'I know Princess Penelope's part cold, Mrs Hunter,'

Cheyenne said. 'And furthermore, Dominique knows *my* part, the part of the compact-fluorescent-bulb fairy queen, cold, and can easily step into my place. Her part, as you know, has few spoken lines, and the lines she does have can easily be given to Marianne. Whereas I don't imagine anyone here knows all *Allie's* lines.' Cheyenne's tone implied that no one would *want* to bother memorizing the evil queen's lines.

And, basically, she was right.

I glanced desperately at Mrs Hunter. Surely she would say, 'Actually, Cheyenne, *I* know Allie's part, and I'll be happy to play the evil queen so that Allie can play Princess Penelope, because she is such a better and more talented actress than you, and we all want her and not you to play the part of the princess. So just pipe down.'

Only Mrs Hunter didn't say that. She looked over at me and asked, 'Well, Allie? Is there anyone you can think of who would be willing to take the part of the evil queen?'

In the last row, where I sat, both Stuart Maxwell and Rosemary swivelled in their chairs to face me, their faces masks of astonished betrayal.

'You *can't* quit playing the evil queen to play the stupid princess,' Rosemary hissed down the row at me. 'That part is so dumb! You're so funny as the evil queen!'

'Yeah,' Stuart whispered. 'And besides, princesses stink!'

And Patrick, down at the very end of our row, leaned forward to whisper, 'Who'll help me with my lines if you're not around as the queen? Huh? Who?'

Beside me, Joey made growling noises, a clear indication he was just upset in general.

Blinking, I put my hand down. As much as I didn't want to admit it, Cheyenne was right. The evil queen *did* have a lot of lines . . . and of course, there wasn't anyone who knew them all, and could – or wanted to – take over my part. It didn't look like Mrs Hunter wanted to.

And so it seemed as if I was stuck playing Queen Melissa the Maleficent whether I wanted to or not. Story of my life.

'That's OK,' I said to Mrs Hunter, even as I saw all my Hollywood dreams slipping down the drain. 'Cheyenne can have the part. I'll just go on playing Queen Mel – I mean, the evil queen.'

'Well,' Mrs Hunter said, 'that's settled then. Why don't we turn our attention to social studies . . .'

So. It was over. I was just going to be plain old Allie Finkle – not Allie Finkle, Superstar, or Allie

Finkle, Best Actress in a Starring Glamorous Role –
forever. Would no one ever recognize that there was
princess potential in me? Or was I going to be stuck
being the evil queen – what Uncle Jay called a character role – for all time?

And OK, it was nice that I was able to make
kindergarteners and my friends and the boys in the
last row of Room 209 laugh.

But it would have been nice to have had my
princess power recognized for once.

And now Cheyenne – bratty, horrible *Cheyenne* –
was going to get what she wanted. *Again.*

And the worst part was, I could see her sitting over
there, looking all pleased with herself, passing notes
to 'M and D'. She really was going to turn into an evil
queen – an *actual one*, who went around murdering
anyone prettier than her – if this kept up. Cheyenne
always got what she wanted . . . high-heeled zip-up
boots, pierced ears, hundred-dollar amethyst
earrings, the most expensive costume, and now the
lead in the play . . .

But wait.

Wait a minute.

She didn't *have* to get this. Not if I had any say in
it.

Because even though no one wanted me to *play* a
princess, that didn't mean I couldn't *act* like one.

Or rather, like a queen.

I knew how to do the queenly thing and save the day. I guess I'd known it all along.

And *When you know the right thing to do, you have to do it*. That's a rule.

Yes. It really *was* all up to me.

I guess I'd always known, in the end, that it would be.

Which was how, after school, instead of going straight on at the Stop sign, I persuaded Erica to turn down Caroline's street. And we all three of us walked to Sophie's house and knocked.

'Oh, hello, girls,' Sophie's mom said when she came to open the door. Sophie's mom was working on her PhD, so as usual, she was dressed in sweats and had a pencil stuck haphazardly into her hair. 'Did you come to check on Sophie? Isn't that sweet of you. She's feeling a bit better. She's up in her room. Why don't you go up to see her?'

'Thank you, Mrs Abramowitz,' we said, and ran up the stairs to Sophie's room.

Sophie was in her nightgown in her canopy bed, rereading a Little House on the Prairie book, one of her favourite comfort series. When we barged into her room without knocking, her cheeks got a little pink, but all she said was, 'Oh, hey, you guys,' in a weak voice.

166

She was still pretending to be sick. I knew she was pretending because nobody gets sick as much as Sophie.

'Sophie,' I said, getting right down to business. Because that's how queens do it. 'We need you to come back to the play. It's an emergency. Cheyenne got the part of Princess Penelope in your place.'

Sophie's dark eyes flashed a little at that. But then she controlled herself and looked back down at her book.

'Well,' she said softly, 'there's nothing I can do about that. Mrs Hunter kicked me out of the play.'

'Only because you were so rude to Allie,' Erica cried. 'Just apologize, and she'll let you back in. I'm sure of it!'

'Yes,' Caroline said, 'I'm sure Mrs Hunter doesn't want Cheyenne to play Princess Penelope. She wants *you* to play her. That's why she picked you and not Cheyenne in the first place. All you have to do is apologize. Just say you're sorry.'

When Sophie looked back up at us again, her eyes were filled with tears.

'Oh, but how can I?' she wailed. 'I want to. You have no idea how much! I feel terrible for the way I acted. I let being the star of the play go to my head. I know I did. I was horrible to you, Allie. You don't know how sorry I am. But it's too late now! I know it is.'

'It's never too late, Sophie,' I said, going over to the

bed and sitting beside her. 'Have your mother call the school. I'm sure Mrs Hunter is still there, getting ready for the open house. You can talk to her, and then when we go to school for the play tonight, you can apologize to me in front of her, I'll forgive you, and everything will be all right.'

'You don't think Cheyenne will be upset?' Sophie asked worriedly. 'I mean, about getting my part and then my showing up and taking it away again?'

'Of course she'll be upset,' I said. 'But who cares? Cheyenne is always upset about something.'

Sophie bit her lip. Then she closed her book and threw back her comforter.

'All right,' she said, 'I'll do it. Because it's true. I really am so, so sorry for the way I acted towards you, Allie.'

'That's all right,' I said. 'I forgive you. That's what friends are for.'

And we all hugged Sophie . . .

. . . even though, if you ask me, she didn't totally deserve our forgiveness. But, being a queen, I forgave her anyway, because it was the queenly thing to do.

Besides, it was for the good of the play, so that's all that mattered.

Rule #13

Nothing Is Impossible If
You Put Your Mind to It.
Nothing at All

It was weird to be in Pine Heights Elementary School at night. It smelt different. It looked different too, somehow. I couldn't really explain how. It was just that, with all the lights on, and the windows dark because it was night outside, you saw how much older things were in a way that you didn't notice so much during the daytime.

Not that this dampened my nervousness in any way. I was carrying my costume, and listening to Mark and Kevin as they chattered away to Mom and Dad and Uncle Jay and Harmony about the presentations their classes were going to put on later in the week (about newts in Mark's case, and in Kevin's a song about rainbows).

'All right,' I said to my family when they got to the auditorium slash gym slash cafeteria doors, where Mr Elkhart had set up tons of folding chairs in front of the stage. We were a little late, so Mrs Jenkins had already begun talking, and it was dark in the auditorium. But it was OK, because Mrs Danielson's class was going first, with the world's most boring presentation on early settlers. I just hoped my parents and Uncle Jay and Harmony wouldn't die of boredom before it was my class's turn to perform. 'You guys go sit down. I have to go to Room two oh nine to get ready. So see you soon.'

'Good luck, honey,' Mom said, bending down to kiss me.

'Never say "good luck" to a performer,' Uncle Jay said. 'Always say "break a leg".' He shook my hand. 'Break a leg, kiddo.'

'Uh, thanks,' I said to him. Why would he want me to break a leg? That sounded awful. Theatre people are just weird.

Then I turned and ran upstairs to Room 209 . . .

. . . which was in chaos. Everyone who didn't already have their costume on was trying to get into one, while everyone who did have their costume on was running around going over their lines or, as in the case of Patrick Day and Stuart Maxwell, having a cardboard sword-fight.

And in the middle of it all, I saw Sophie and Cheyenne standing in front of Mrs Hunter, both with tears in their eyes.

Uh-oh.

I spotted Caroline and Erica standing nearby, already in costume, and hurried over to them.

'What's going on?' I asked them, nodding my head towards Cheyenne and Sophie.

'Sophie told Mrs Hunter she was sorry for what she'd done and wanted to come back and be in the play,' Erica said breathlessly. 'And that she'd apologized to you, and we said we all witnessed it. Then Sophie asked Mrs Hunter if she could have her part back. But Cheyenne overheard, and came rushing over and said she won't give the part of Princess Penelope up!'

'Oh no!' I bit my lip. This was awful! I knew it was up to me to make things right. Somehow.

I dashed over to the little cluster by the chalkboard. 'Mrs Hunter,' I said. 'It's true. Sophie apologized to me. And I've forgiven her. We're friends again. *Please* let Sophie back into the play.'

Mrs Hunter looked down at me as I stood there. I'd reached for Sophie's hand, because I'd seen that she had tears in her eyes and seemed as close to fainting as I'd ever seen her (Sophie is a bit of a dramatic fainter). She didn't say anything, but I could read the *Thank-you* in her eyes as they gleamed tearfully back at me. As chaotic as Room 209 had been before, it now got very quiet. You could hear Mrs Danielson's class putting on their boring presentation downstairs, that's how quiet it was: *And in olden times, they didn't have things like nice, sanitary water fountains. Everyone shared the same dipper from the same old-timey well. And that's how they all got cholera.*

'Mrs Hunter,' Cheyenne said, interrupting the silence, 'you said *I* could have the part of Princess Penelope!'

'Yes,' Mrs Hunter said, 'but that was when Sophie wasn't feeling well. She's obviously better now, and she's apologized to Allie. She and I agreed if she did that, she could come back to the play. Remember, Cheyenne?'

So! It turned out that all Sophie had to do all along to get back into the play was apologize to me. Nice of her to let us know.

Cheyenne's eyes got very narrow as she glared at Mrs Hunter. I could tell she was getting ready to say *Shut up*, just like she had to her mother that day in the mall.

Only Cheyenne didn't dare say shut up to Mrs Hunter. *No one would ever say shut up to Mrs Hunter. Not if they wanted to live to see tomorrow.* That's a rule.

'That's not *fair*,' Cheyenne said instead, stamping her foot.

'Well, you're not the director of this production,' Mrs Hunter said, her green eyes beginning to crackle, a dangerous sign that she was getting angry, 'are you, Cheyenne?'

Cheyenne looked like she was going to argue for a second . . . but then realized that she wasn't actually the director of Mrs Hunter's play. When this finally sunk in, she got a sour look on her face . . .

. . . then stuck her nose in the air and flounced away.

Mrs Hunter turned to Sophie and said with a smile, 'I'm glad you're feeling better.'

'Thank you, Mrs Hunter,' Sophie said, her face brightening. She'd finally realized she was going to get to play Princess Penelope after all. 'Thank you so much! And again, I'm really, really sorry.'

'That's all right, Sophie,' Mrs Hunter said. 'We all have our bad days. Now you'd better go finish getting ready.'

'I will, Mrs Hunter,' Sophie said. She let go of my hand and ran, with a delighted squeal, over to hug Caroline and Erica.

To me, Mrs Hunter said quietly, 'Thank you for being so understanding, Allie. You've really been very mature and professional about all this.'

I felt myself blushing with pleasure at this unexpected compliment. Professional! Mrs Hunter thought I'd been a mature professional!

That was practically like saying next time our

class did a play with a princess in it, Mrs Hunter was going to give the part to me. Wasn't it?

'Now, hadn't you better go put your costume on?' Mrs Hunter said. 'We're supposed to perform at seven thirty, right after Mrs Danielson's class. You'd better hurry.'

'Right away, Mrs Hunter,' I said. I hugged my costume to myself. Mature! And professional! Me!

I took my costume and hurried off to the girls' room to put it on, not stopping to join the other girls in their little celebration. I hadn't told anyone, but I'd made a special adjustment to Queen Melissa the Maleficent's look, and I needed extra time to get it just right. No, I hadn't traded in my red high-tops. It was something else, and it was supposed to be a surprise. I wanted to see if anyone noticed. It took a while for me to get it right, though – longer than I thought it would. Caroline, Rosemary and Erica each came into the girls' room once to tell me to hurry up.

Finally, though, I got my costume exactly the way I wanted it. And when I came out, our class was already lining up to go downstairs to perform.

'Hey, what did you do?' Rosemary whispered when I got in line. 'You look different.'

'Nothing,' I said innocently.

'No,' Rosemary said, 'you did something.'

'I didn't,' I whispered. But I was telling a lie. Just a little one. A fib, basically. 'Do you think I look good?'

'I don't know. Maybe. Tell me what you did and I'll tell you if you look good.'

'Fine,' I said. I pointed to my eyes. 'False eyelashes.'

Rosemary stared. 'Really? They look real. But bigger.'

'Yeah,' I said. 'I borrowed them from my mom.'

'Cool,' Rosemary said.

'Girls,' Mrs Hunter said from the front of the line. 'Shh.'

So we had to stop talking. Our class went down the stairs to where all the parents were waiting. We could hear them clapping in the gym for the class that had gone ahead of ours . . . Mrs Danielson's presentation on early settlers. I couldn't believe they were clapping so much for something I personally knew to be so boring.

'All right, everybody,' Mrs Hunter said. We were all gathered by the secret door that led to the backstage area, so no one would see us going into the auditorium and setting up the stage behind the curtains for our show. 'I want you to do the best you can tonight. Don't be nervous. Remember it's only your families out there, and they love you. You're going to be great . . .'

'Hey,' Sophie said, coming to stand right next to

me, 'I just wanted to say again that I'm sorry I acted like such a brat. Can you forgive me?'

'Of course,' I said. I wasn't lying either. I guess we can all let things go to our head sometimes. Not everyone can be a mature professional like me.

'What did you do to your eyes?' Sophie wanted to know.

'False eyelashes,' I whispered.

'Really?' She looked impressed. 'That's so cool.'

'Thanks,' I said. So Sophie really *had* had a major attitude adjustment since Mrs Hunter had kicked her out of the play, then let her back in.

'. . . and most of all,' Mrs Hunter went on, 'I want you to break a leg. Got it?'

'Got it,' we all said. Even though of course none of us understood where that crazy expression had come from.

'Good,' she said, and opened the door to backstage.

We all went as quietly as we could behind the stage to get our assigned set pieces and put them where they belonged, while out on the stage, Mrs Jenkins introduced us.

'And now,' the principal said, 'Mrs Hunter's fourth-grade class, Room two oh nine, would like to present an original play, *Princess Penelope in the Realm of Recycling*.'

STAGE FRIGHT

We all ran off the stage so that only Sophie was left there, in her spot, to deliver her first line when the curtain opened. Which she did, as soon as the spotlight, operated by Mr Elkhart, hit her.

If she was nervous, you couldn't tell. *I* was sure nervous, as I stood in the wings. There were *a lot* more people out there than there'd been that morning, when we'd been performing for the kindergarteners. I could hear them rustling around, moving their legs and their programmes, coughing and whispering. I could see some of them too, though not my family. It was too dark for me to make out individual faces.

When Sophie said the line that was my cue to come out on stage, I suddenly felt a huge wave of nervousness come over me. What was I doing? I couldn't do this! I was too scared! What if I messed up and forgot my lines?

On the other hand . . . I had practised so much! I knew all my lines and everyone else's too. I wasn't going to mess up.

And if I did, I knew Uncle Jay and my parents would forgive me. Because like Mrs Hunter had said, they loved me. Just like I had forgiven Sophie for being such a brat earlier that day.

And besides, why was I even nervous? Queens don't get nervous.

Especially evil queens. And that's who I was now. Not Allie Finkle, but a very, very evil queen. I just had to remember that.

So I went out on to the stage, doing my special evil-queen walk and talking in my special Queen Melissa the Maleficent voice (which was a mix of Missy and Cheyenne – but mostly Cheyenne, even if she didn't know it).

And right away, before I'd even fully delivered my first line, everyone started laughing.

Just like Kevin had said. Basically, I was awesome.

And all my nervousness went away. Acting was really fun! It was great to make people laugh! It was even more fun making grown-ups laugh than kinder-garteners. For one thing, grown-ups laughed a lot louder and harder than little kids did.

Also, you barely had to do anything to make adults laugh. It was amazing! I had the place in an uproar in no time. I really wasn't expecting that. I expected a *little* laughter, on account of my shoes and socks.

But not *this*.

Maybe it was the eyelashes.

Or maybe it was relief on the audience's part that we weren't doing a presentation on early settlers.

Or maybe it was just that I was such a mature pro-fessional.

But whatever the reason, the audience seemed to love the play . . . all of it.

Even Cheyenne, who didn't flit around with quite as much abandon as she had that morning. But she definitely put a lot more effort than usual into it.

And when I'd finished my death scene and lay sprawled across the stage with my red high-tops in the air, struck dead by my own pollution ray . . . well, we got a huge standing ovation.

I actually felt a little sorry for all the classes who were going to have to follow ours, later in the week. How would they ever top Room 209's performance?

After the curtains closed, we all let out a big scream of excitement before Mrs Hunter herded us back upstairs to our classroom to wait until our parents came to get us.

'You were so good,' Sophie said as she hugged me.

'You were better,' I told her.

'No,' she said, 'you were.'

'Oh, we were all good,' Erica said, hugging both of us. 'Even Cheyenne.'

We all had to agree.

And because we were still practising positive re-inforcement in the hopes it would make Cheyenne a nicer person, we even told her we thought she'd been good. But she only made a face at us and said, 'Um, I *know*.'

It was right after that that our families came to find us. All the parents were full of compliments for Mrs Hunter on the wonderful show. Even Mr and Mrs O'Malley, Cheyenne's mom and dad.

'I'm so glad you liked it,' Mrs Hunter said. She didn't say anything more, like that Cheyenne was a joy to have in the classroom, or that she was a mature professional, like she'd said about me. Because she'd have been lying if she said that about Cheyenne.

Finally my own parents came to get me. Mark, Kevin, Uncle Jay and Harmony were tagging along behind them.

'You were so great!' Dad said, giving me a congratulatory hug. 'Don't tell any of the other kids,' he whispered in my ear, 'but you were the best one.'

'I definitely want to write about this play,' Harmony said, 'for my topical seminar in media and society. It had an intriguing premise.'

'I knew you had it in you all along, kid,' Uncle Jay said, giving me another handshake when Dad put me down. 'You're a natural.'

'Thanks,' I said modestly.

'Oh, Allie, you were very, very funny,' Mom said. And then her voice trailed off. 'Allie . . . what's that on your . . .? Allie! Are you wearing a pair of my false eyelashes?'

'Yes,' I said. Shoot. I'd forgotten to take them off before she got there. 'I didn't think you'd mind. They're to make my eyes look bigger on stage. I mean, you wear them on TV, so I thought—'

'Allie Finkle,' Mom said, 'you march into the bathroom and take those off right now. You are too young to be wearing those. And taking something of mine without asking! I'm ashamed of you!'

I couldn't believe she was yelling at me in front of everybody.

But I guess I did kind of deserve it. One of the rules in our house is *Don't take anything that doesn't belong to you without asking first.*

Which was why I hadn't asked, since I'd known she'd say no.

As I peeled off the eyelashes, I stared at myself thoughtfully in the mirror over the sinks. To think that I, Allie Finkle, had just that evening been in a hit play. And had caused so many people to laugh so hard! It was obvious they'd really enjoyed it. Erica's dad, Mr Harrington, had told me I'd been the best part of the whole night, and Erica's brother John had said he'd never seen anything funnier than my death scene in his whole life.

Even Missy had put down her cellphone long enough to grunt at me and say, 'You were OK.'

Those had to be good things, right?

It was true that I hadn't gotten to play the part I'd wanted. I hadn't gotten famous (yet), or gotten a limo or bodyguards or paparazzi following me around.

I hadn't been a sore loser, like Cheyenne, and I hadn't let my part go to my head, like Sophie.

But I'd done my best with the part I'd gotten.

And Uncle Jay said that was the sign of a truly dedicated performer.

And Mrs Hunter had said I'd acted like a mature professional.

What's more, I'd learned something really important: I liked acting. I was feeling really, really good right now (except for the part about Mom's eyelashes). But about the show, about the nice things people had said to me afterwards . . . and about acting as a career choice in general.

I wonder how hard it would be to be both an actress *and* a veterinarian.

It would be difficult, I bet, to do both.

But not impossible.

If anything, this whole thing had proved the rule that *Nothing is impossible if you put your mind to it.*

Nothing at all.

Allie Finkle's Rules

- Never eat anything red.
- Don't chew with your mouth open.
- Swallow what's in your mouth before speaking.
- It's important to try to make your friends feel good about themselves as often as possible. Then they'll like you better.
- Popularity isn't important. Being a kind and thoughtful person is.
- Cheyenne is officially boring.
- There's no kissing in fourth grade.
- You should always tell people they look nice, even when they don't. This makes people feel good, so they'll like you better.
- It's rude to tell someone they're only going to get something because no one else wants it, not because they earned it.
- Don't play tackle football in the hallway.
- Don't slam doors in people's faces.

- Whenever possible, try to be born into a family with no little brothers.
- May the best man – or woman – win.
- It's wrong to hate people.
- Practice makes perfect.
- It's always better to have things out in the open than to let them fester.
- The best way to keep a person from getting mad at you is to compliment them. Even if you don't think it's true.
- If you want to get anywhere, you can't play by the rules.
- You are supposed to answer the phone politely.
- Friends try to make friends feel better.
- Friends don't try to make friends feel bad on purpose.
- No one likes a sore loser.
- No one likes a sore winner.
- You can celebrate all you want in private, where the losers can't see you.
- There are no small parts. Only small actors.
- It's rude to interrupt people.
- If you whine about it, you'll get sent to your room and also have your TV privileges suspended and maybe also no dessert and possibly also your Nintendo DS taken away for a week.

STAGE FRIGHT

- Best friends rescue each other when someone's evil sister has them trapped.
- You can't make someone with a bad attitude about something change their mind and have a good one. You just can't.
- Treat people the way you yourself would like to be treated.
- It's OK to lie if the lie makes someone else feel better.
- Make the best of it.
- When you know the right thing to do, you have to do it.
- No one would ever say shut up to Mrs Hunter. Not if they wanted to live to see tomorrow.
- Don't take anything that doesn't belong to you without asking first.
- Nothing is impossible if you put your mind to it. Nothing at all.

So what happens next to Allie?

Find out in . . .

ALLIE FINKLE'S
RULES
FOR
GIRLS
GLITTER GIRLS

Read the first chapter over the page

Rule #1

It's Important to Try Not to Hurt Someone's Feelings If You Can Help It

'Is that the one you're going to wear?' I stared at the red spangled bodysuit Erica's older sister Missy had on.

I could hardly believe how beautiful she looked in it. Usually when I saw Missy she had on sweatpants.

Sweatpants and a really mean expression as she was slamming her bedroom door in my face.

It wouldn't be an exaggeration to say that Missy hated my guts.

But then Missy hated the guts of all Erica's friends, so I didn't take it personally. Missy hated Erica too, even though Erica refused to believe it, and was always trying to do nice things for her big sister.

Like right now, for instance, Erica had enlisted our help in getting Missy to decide which of her six fanciest baton-twirling costumes she should wear for the seventh annual Little Miss Majorette Baton Twirling Twirltacular, middle-school division.

'I think you should wear the blue one,' Rosemary said.

'The blue one doesn't have as much glitter,' Sophie said from Missy's bed, where we were sitting all in a row while Missy was putting on her fashion show for us. 'Only sparkly fringe.'

This was the first time we'd ever been invited into Missy's bedroom after school, so it was truly a huge occasion, and we were trying very hard not to break the rules Missy had explained to us before she'd allowed us to come in.

The rules were 1) *Do not touch anything*, 2) *No talking unless Missy says you can talk*, and 3) *Leave the minute Missy says so*.

Break the rules, and Missy would break you.

'I know,' Rosemary said. 'That's why I like the blue one.'

'The red one is definitely sparklier,' Caroline said. 'Although sparklier isn't a word.'

Caroline would know. She was our class spelling champion, even though she lost the district spelling bee.

'I just can't decide,' Missy said with a sigh as she

fluffed out her blonde hair and stared at herself in her full-length mirror. 'I do look amazing in all of them, don't I?'

'Yes,' we all said in unison.

Always agree with everything Missy says if you want her to stay in a good mood. This was another rule.

Being friends with Erica was very good training for how to deal with teenagers. Also how not to act when I become one. Because Missy was really moody. Also rude. At least most of the time. She was being nice to us today though, because she wanted our help deciding what to wear to the Little Miss Majorette Baton Twirling Twirltacular.

I won't lie: I wanted to go to the Little Miss Majorette Baton Twirling Twirltacular more than I had ever wanted to go anywhere in my whole entire life. At least, ever since I'd heard about it (half an hour earlier).

Because Missy and Erica and Mrs Harrington (who had hand-sewn all Missy's costumes for her) had told us about it while we'd been eating after-school snacks of fruit and graham crackers in the kitchen of their house.

And it sounded like the most exciting thing in the world.

First of all, twirlers (that's what the people who spin and toss batons are called. Twirlers. Also majorettes, but twirler is more correct because a twirler can be a boy *or* a girl, whereas majorettes are only girls) come from all over the state – possibly even from *outside* the state – to participate in the Twirltacular, which lasts a whole weekend.

At the Twirltacular, there are events in dance, strut, teams, show twirls, solos, multiple batons, flags, hoops and duets/pairs.

I don't exactly know what any of that means, but I totally want to see it. In fact, the more I heard about it from Erica and Mrs Harrington and Missy, the more I thought I would *die* if I didn't get to see it.

And I was really lucky, because the Little Miss Majorette Baton Twirling Twirltacular was happening right here in my *very own town*.

Missy said if we didn't act like ingrates, which means an ungrateful person, we could come watch her compete.

So there was a chance I might actually get to see her perform at the Little Miss Majorette Baton Twirling Twirltacular, middle-school division. My friends Sophie, Caroline and I decided that we were going to go with Erica on Saturday, in order to show our support for her sister.

Our friend Rosemary wasn't sure if she wanted to go or not. She thought twirling sounded very boring, despite all the sparkles.

But of course she didn't say so in front of Missy, because that would hurt Missy's feelings.

It's important to try not to hurt someone's feelings if you can help it. That's a rule.

It's especially important to try not to hurt Missy's feelings, because she is much bigger than we are, and when you do something she doesn't like, she'll tackle you and sit on you and then spit in your face. She's done this to me before and it was really gross.

Missy's parents, Mr and Mrs Harrington, were going to the Little Miss Majorette Baton Twirling Twirltacular of course. So was John, Erica and Missy's older brother. At first, Erica said, John didn't want to go. Like Rosemary, John thought twirling was boring.

But then after John saw Missy's leotards, he asked if there'd be any girls his own age at the event, and Mrs Harrington said yes there would be, since the competition went from sixth to eighth grade, which was John's grade.

So then John said maybe he might like to go after all.

The grand prizewinners in each event at the Twirltacular, Missy said, get a trophy that's as big as I am. At the top of the trophy is a statue of a little gold lady twirling a baton (if you're a boy twirler, you get a little gold man, Missy said, although she doubted there would be any boy twirlers at the Little Miss Majorette Baton Twirling Twirltacular).

I wanted Missy to get one of these trophies. I wanted her to get one very, very much.

And I wanted to be there when she got it. I wanted to be there to help support her, to cheer her on and to eat the popcorn that Erica said they always sell in little paper bags at the middle school whenever they had these events. *Good News!*, the local cable television news show where my mother does movie reviews, might even be there to report on the event. They came last year, Erica said.

'I think you should wear the lime-green one with the rhinestone fringe,' Erica said to Missy. 'And the rainbow one with the purple glitter.'

'That's my favourite,' Sophie said, sounding as if her heart was aching because she wanted to have a rainbow-coloured leotard, covered in sequins, with a purple glittery fringe dangling down from the leg holes.

I knew how Sophie felt, because I felt exactly the

same way. I wanted one of those baton-twirling costumes, even though I don't know how to twirl a baton (although I've practised a bit in the front yard with one of Missy's old batons that she doesn't use any more. The problem was, the baton fell down from the tree where I accidentally threw it, and hit me on the head. After that I decided just to stick with ballet, which I do on Saturdays and also on Wednesdays after school, and softball in the Girls Club team in the summertime).

'Yeah,' Missy said thoughtfully, baring her teeth and examining her electric-blue braces in the mirror. 'I think you guys are right. I'll wear the rainbow one for my dance routine, and the green one for my solo.'

Then Missy signalled to Erica to turn on her CD player. And so Erica did. Missy's song for her twirling solo came on, and Missy started practising it in the mirror. The song was called 'I'm Gonna Knock You Out', and it was playing very, very loud.

So loud that I'm sure Sophie thought Missy couldn't hear her when she leaned over to whisper to us, 'You guys, we *have* to go see Missy perform on Saturday.'

Erica looked over at her sister, whose back was to us as she performed in front of the mirror. 'Shh,' she said in a panicky way. 'She'll hear you! She said no talking, remember?'

'I know,' Sophie said. 'But I just think it's really important we all go on Saturday. To support Missy. I think she has problems with her self-esteem. That's why she's so bossy. Allie, are you able to go? Don't ou have ballet on Saturday?'

I had forgotten I had ballet with Madame Linda on Saturday. My parents pay in advance for my lessons too.

'That's OK,' I said. 'I'm sure I can skip my lesson this one time.'

This was a lie. But it was just a very small lie. I was sure it didn't matter. Very much.

'That's good,' Sophie said. 'What about you, Caroline?'

'Oh, I can go,' Caroline said. 'I have my Mandarin lesson, but it's just with my dad. I can do it any time.'

'You guys,' Rosemary said when she saw we were all looking at her. 'I don't want to go. And I don't think anything is wrong with Missy's self-esteem. She's just a brat. And baton twirling is boring.'

'It's not boring,' Sophie said, looking offended. 'It's a very beautiful form of self-expression.'

'Missy is kind of bossy,' Erica admitted. 'But she doesn't have very many friends. She could really use our support.'

'Teenage hormones,' Caroline said knowingly. 'I've read about this. You're right. We have to support her.'

It was kind of funny that right at that moment Missy turned round and, looking enraged, yelled, 'I said no talking!'

We all knew what was coming next. We jumped from Missy's bed and ran for her bedroom door before she could leap on any of us, knock us down and sit on us.

Thinking about what might happen after that was too terrible even to contemplate.

Fortunately we all made it out into the safety of the hallway, where Mrs Harrington happened to be walking by with another of Missy's twirling costumes. She had been hemming it down in her studio, where she also made fine collectibles, such as doll's house furniture and miniature felt toadstools with tiny lady dwarfs sitting on them, to sell in her shop downtown.

'Good heavens!' Mrs Harrington said when we all came tumbling out of Missy's room at the same time. 'What's going on?'

'Nothing,' we chimed together, coming to a halt right in front of her.

When Missy saw her mom, she pointed an accusing finger at us and said, 'That's not true! I was performing my dance routine for Saturday, and they started talking! It broke my concentration.'

'Well, honey,' Mrs Harrington said, completely unruffled, though Missy looked as if she was about to cry. Really! She had tears in her eyes and everything (except that they were fake tears, if you ask me), 'I'm sure the girls didn't mean any disrespect. And you're going to have to get used to people talking during your performances. There are going to be all sorts of distractions this weekend. People talking, other girls and boys doing their routines at the same time yours is going on.' Also, people eating popcorn. 'You're really going to need to learn how to focus and block them all out, sweetie.'

Our eyes wide, we all glanced over at Missy to see how she'd handle this information. She narrowed her eyes at her mother, then fixed each of us with a glare that could have melted snow.

Then, she turned round and stormed back into her room, slamming the door behind her.

'Excuse me,' Mrs Harrington called after her, 'but we *Do not slam doors* around here, young lady!'

11

This was a rule.

'Sorry,' Missy called from inside her room.

But if you ask me, she didn't sound sorry at all.

'I'm sorry about that, Mrs Harrington,' Rosemary said. Rosemary was very good about apologizing to adults. 'We didn't mean to make Missy upset. And those glittery costumes you made for her are awfully nice.'

'Why, thank you, Rosemary!' Mrs Harrington beamed. 'I'm very flattered you like them. If you'd like to take up twirling, I'd be happy to make you one as well. Twirling's such a lovely sport. I think any one of you girls would be very good at it.'

The idea of Rosemary, whose favourite sport was football – especially the part where you got to tackle people and hold them to the ground – daintily prancing around a dance floor while spinning a baton was so hilarious that for a minute it was all I could do to keep myself from bursting out laughing.

But I controlled myself.

'Thank you, Mrs Harrington,' Rosemary said. 'But that's OK. In fact, I think I have to be going now. My mom's going to be coming to pick me up soon.'

'Oh, I have to go too,' I said.

'Why?' Erica looked disappointed.

'Because I have to ask my mom about skipping ballet on Saturday, so I can go to the Little Miss Majorette Baton Twirling Twirltacular.'

I knew my mom wouldn't like my missing my ballet lesson. Neither would Madame Linda, who was super strict, and sometimes smacked us on the thigh if we didn't properly turn them out during ronds de jambe en l'air (this used to make my ex-best friend Mary Kay Shiner cry, so she quit coming to Madame Linda's. But then, everything made Mary Kay Shiner cry, so this was no big surprise).

But Madame Linda's disapproval when I skipped Saturday's lesson would be completely worth it.

Especially if I got to be there when Missy ended up winning one of those giant trophies she'd told us about!

When I got home, I saw Dad first, sitting at the dining-room table, which he uses as his office, grading tests from the computer-science class he teaches.

But I knew better than to ask him if it was OK if I skipped ballet class to go to Missy's Little Miss Majorette Baton Twirling Twirltacular on Saturday.

Because he would just say, 'Fine,' like he did about everything.

And it would *seem* fine. Until Mom found out.

And then it would turn out it *wasn't* fine. It was always better to ask Mom first. About *everything*.

'Mom,' I said when I found her in her bedroom, putting things in a suitcase. This was so startling – my parents never go anywhere – that I completely forgot what I'd been about to say, and went, 'Where are you going?'

'Oh, honey,' Mom said, brushing some hair from her eyes, 'you know. I told you. Daddy and I are going to Cousin Freddie's wedding at Grandma and Grandpa's house this weekend in San Francisco. Pass me that shirt, will you?'

I passed her one of Dad's shirts, which sat folded on the bed. I'd forgotten that she and Dad were going to Cousin Freddie's wedding. I'd only met my mom's cousin Freddie once, at a family reunion at the country club where my grandma and grandpa on my mom's side live in California. Cousin Freddie had let me and Mark drive his golf cart, even though we weren't really big enough to reach the pedals.

It wasn't our fault we accidentally drove the golf cart on to the tennis courts of the country club. No one had been too happy about this, especially

Grandpa, who'd yelled at Cousin Freddie for a long time.

'What is it you wanted to ask me, Allie?' Mom wanted to know.

'Oh,' I said. 'Well, Missy Harrington is going to compete in the seventh annual Little Miss Majorette Baton Twirling Twirltacular, middle-school division, on Saturday, and I really, really want to go. I know I have ballet that morning, but I promise I'll make up my missed lesson over the summer. Erica and Caroline and Sophie and probably Rosemary are all going. We think it's important that we go to support Missy, who is suffering from self-esteem issues, and hardly has any friends due to her teenage hormones. Also, I think I'll learn positive messages there about teamwork, camaraderie and the spirit of competitive-ness.'

I had gotten that last part from a book I'd checked out from the school library about female horse jockeys. There wouldn't be any female horse jockeys at the annual Little Miss Majorette Baton Twirling Twirltacular. But I thought the thing about teamwork and competitiveness sounded good anyway.

'Twirltacular?' My little brother Kevin looked up from Mom and Dad's bed, where he was reading a fancy furniture catalogue that had come in the mail.

Kevin liked to collect fancy furniture catalogues. 'I want to go to Missy's Twirltacular.'

'Well, you're not invited,' I said. Kevin was always trying to hang around with my friends. He thought they liked him as much as they liked me, which wasn't true actually.

'Oh dear,' Mom said. 'Is Missy's competition is this coming Saturday?'

'Yes,' I said. 'But I'm sure Uncle Jay won't mind.'

'Uncle Jay's not—' Kevin started to say, but Mom interrupted him, even though one of the rules at our house is *Don't interrupt people*.

'Honey, I forgot to tell you,' Mom said. 'This Saturday is Brittany Hauser's birthday party. And she's invited you. And I'm afraid I already told her mother that you'd go.'